MW01256997

CITY SHIFTERS: THE PRIDE

BOOK I

Thrill of the Chase

LAYLA NASH

Copyright © 2015 by Layla Nash

All rights reserved.

No part of this book may be reproduced in any form or by any electronic or mechanical means, including information storage and retrieval systems, without written permission from the author, except for the use of brief quotations in a book review.

Cover design by
Resplendent Media

Interior book design by
Write Dream Repeat Book Design LLC

chapter 1

The kitchen was slammed for dinner, despite having only ten tables, and as my sous chef scrambled to plate dishes before anything cooled, I faced off with the manager through the door of his office. "We're out of tuna. There were at least twenty steaks in the cooler yesterday, and now there's nothing. What the hell happened, Joey?"

He leaned his chair back, the squeak grating on my ears even with the din of the kitchen in the background. "I'm sure you miscounted."

"Fuck you, I can count." I slammed my fist into the door jamb. "I cannot run this kitchen if my inventory disappears whenever one of your shitbag friends shows up."

"Slow your roll, sweetheart." He got up, eyes narrowed, and tried to loom over me. His five foot six was no match for my five ten, though, and I folded my arms over my chest. It also helped that I had a scary large butcher knife in my hand. The manager glanced behind me, then raised an eyebrow. "Don't concern yourself with this fictional tuna. My guy will be here in a couple days with fresh. Go take care of your own business."

My teeth ground until pain spiked in my temples. "I swear to God, Joey, if this doesn't stop, I'm quitting. I'll walk the fuck away."

"Go ahead and try." His dark eyes studied me, his voice low and tense. "See how far Bob lets you run. Just remember where you started, sweetheart." He reached out, trailing his knuckles across my cheek, and I jerked back.

"If you ever touch me again," I said, butcher knife held even with his chin. "I will gut you like the swine you are. I butchered a whole cow in school, Joey. You're not even a challenge."

We faced off, neither of us looking away. I wondered if I would have to kick him in the junk to get him to back down, but instead my sous chef, Jake, called from behind me. "Chef, get your ass back in here, we need a hand with the special."

I scowled at the manager, "Get better vendors, for fuck's sake, all of your friends have shitty product," and turned to storm back into the kitchen.

Jake took one look at my face and directed me to where one of the line cooks tenderized the steaks, so I pounded my rage out on the beef with a meat hammer. It didn't help much, except when I imagined Joey's ugly, narrow face under the spikes. I'd almost worked off the fury at the missing tuna and Joey's casual disregard for my menu planning when one of the waiters crept into the kitchen.

He pitched his voice over the hiss and pop of the sauté pans. "Chef? A guest asked to speak with you."

"Which guest?"

"The one who sent back his steak."

My lip curled in disgust. He sent back a perfectly prepared filet and claimed I did not know medium rare. The steak was perfect — I'd inspected it myself before it went out. I waved my towel at the server and took over preparing the hollandaise from the young saucier, not wanting to end up with scrambled eggs. "I do not have time to listen to his apology."

"Chef, he wanted to send it back again."

I dropped the bowl and hollandaise splattered across my apron and the rest of the workstation. "Again? I prepared that steak myself."

The waiter offered only an expressive shrug, taking no responsibility for the man's lack of taste. I gritted my teeth; no one ever said customers would take up this much time for a head chef. On a normal night, I probably could have pretended and listened to the man's complaint without wanting to snap my towel in his face, but after the confrontation with Joey... The towel twisted in my hands. I didn't like people. That was why I worked with food.

Jake wiped up the spilled sauce as he said under his breath, "Don't go out there unless you can be civil. We need every paying customer."

"That steak was perfect."

Jake sighed. "We just got the lights turned back on. Is it worth it?"

"This is my kitchen," I said, taking a step back as anger bubbled up still more. It was bad enough I had to deal with chauvinist pigs in every kitchen as I worked my way up, and that I had to fight to be taken seriously by my vendors and my staff and the competition up and down this trendy street. Even worse that Joey sold my inventory out from under me whenever he wanted. Now some jackass who wanted to eat my food insulted me in front of my entire kitchen and the other guests. "I'm supposed to send out another steak?"

He shook his head, concentrating on the other dishes being plated. "Very well. I will keep everything else going. Go alienate some of our paying customers."

I muttered about his family tree under my breath as I stormed out of the kitchen, still wearing the splattered apron and pristine chef's coat, my hair covered with a thick bandanna. I wiped my hands on the towel as I followed the server, the young man hustling to the problem table. I should have known who it would be as the server paused at a table with five men, all wearing expensive suits and designer ties. Well-groomed. Big and strong, probably from an over-priced trainer at a fancy gym. Alpha males accustomed to getting their way in everything. Well. This was my restaurant, my domain.

The waiter tilted his head at the complainant for my benefit, though he half-bowed and gestured at me as he addressed the man. "Sir, the chef."

"Took long enough," he said, turning slightly in his chair to look at me. By his expression, whatever he saw surprised him — no doubt that I was young, that I was female, that I was pissed as hell. Something changed in his face.

I arched an eyebrow, putting on an imperious facade that had saved me from the attention of every male student at every culinary school I'd attended. He was unfortunately handsome, hard-eyed with a strong jaw and blonde hair a little too long and shaggy for my taste. I slapped the towel against my palm, and when I spoke, a French accent tinged my words — earned the hard way after years of culinary school in France. "Leonard tells me you have something to say. About my food."

"Yes." He touched the edge of his plate, where the steak sat in a bloody puddle. Perfectly grilled, seasoned, aromatic. From a butcher who purchased local meat raised in the Kobe style. Well marbled, aged, tenderized. The cows practically got massages and therapists. And yet this man, this corporate raider who gazed coolly at me as if I worked for him, sat back in his chair and gestured to dismiss all that work. "It's over done. I sent it back once already and expected it to be done correctly. And yet — here we are. I thought it best to tell you exactly how to prepare it."

The blood boiled in my veins, and I twisted the towel before smacking it against my palm again. His companions glanced at each other, then at me. One grinned openly and leaned his elbows on the table like a naughty kid. I shifted my weight and leaned forward, head tilted as I studied him. Smug bastard. "I am so sorry; I did not realize you attended Le Cordon Bleu. When did you graduate?"

"I didn't —"

"Oh, my mistake, it must be the Culinary Institute of America, no?" The French accent grew stronger, and his expression darkened. I threw my hands up. "No, perhaps not the Culinary Institute. That explains it all, certainly."

"Explains what?" he said, grim. Pale brown eyes narrowed as he studied me from head to toe. Not entertained at all, despite that all four of his friends grinned and looked back and forth between us in delight, as if it were a high-stakes tennis match.

"It explains," I said in a lower voice as the other diners began paying attention. It was a very small restaurant, after all. Boutique. "How you did not recognize that both of those steaks were perfectly prepared. Impeccable."

His hands braced on the table, massive paws with long blunt fingers and a neat manicure. "I asked for medium rare, they were —"

"They were perfectly medium rare," I said, the words escaping in something close to a hiss. Too much, because he sat up, lines gathering around his mouth as he frowned. I held my hands up. "Perhaps you have never had a steak this good; perhaps you do not recognize quality when you see it. This is your burden to bear."

His friend, dark haired and younger, smiled at me with even, white teeth, but spoke to the complainant. "Logan, the steak is amazing, just —"

"The steak is over-done," he said, sharp, and the kid sat back, shaking his head. The blonde turned back to me, frown deepening to a scowl. "I want medium rare. I'll keep sending it back until it is done correctly."

I picked up the plate, pretending to examine the steak, and then shrugged. I handed it to the server and jerked my head at the kitchen, where Jake and the rest of the staff watched through the window. When the waiter was on his way, I glanced back at the entitled asshole. "If you cannot appreciate the quality of the food I prepare, or the talent with which I prepare it, you should not eat it."

"I beg your pardon?"

"You must not understand me." I faked concern as the towel swung in a wide gesture. I folded my arms over my chest and looked pointedly at the door. "Get out."

His eyebrows climbed to his hairline and the man across the table burst out laughing. Logan, the corporate raider, looked incredulous to the point of not being able to speak, though he managed to grind out, "What?"

I looked at his friend, still laughing, and pointed at his plate. "You enjoy your ravioli, no?"

"Yes ma'am," the friend said, holding up his hands in surrender. "Delicious and perfectly prepared. *Merci.*"

"*De rien*, I am pleased you enjoy it." I looked back at Logan, who still stared at me as if I'd grown a second head. Perhaps no one had ever rejected him before, maybe in his normal day everyone jumped through their ass to appease him. Not here. Not in my restaurant. "So. Your friends appreciate my work, and yet clearly you cannot. You are welcome to sit as your friends enjoy their food, or you may leave. But I will not waste my time, or my staff's time, preparing yet another meal for you."

I turned on my heel and strode to the kitchen, not looking back as the rest of the patrons applauded. I threw the towel against the wall once behind the door and ignored Jake's long-suffering expression. He read off the remaining orders and started talking about the soufflé. The only thing that could pull me out of a foul mood was cooking, but I couldn't forget the jackass still sitting in my restaurant, insulting my life's work by his very presence, and the malevolent toad in the manager's office.

Even an hour later as Carter and Atticus stuffed themselves with decadent chocolate soufflés, Logan couldn't believe what happened. That damn chef *yelled* at him. Refused to make him a steak. A perfectly unreasonable slip of a woman, spitting mad before he had a chance to explain himself. His brothers practically rolled around in his irritation, celebrating that someone finally put the alpha in his place, and he could do nothing about it. It set his teeth on edge.

Edgar, grave as usual, studied the half-finished glass of wine he'd been nursing all night. "Is there a plan already, Logan? A specific target?"

He put the chef out of his mind, though she was like a sore tooth — he kept going back around to her, probing the irritation to see whether it still bothered him. And it still did. His stomach growled, and Benedict grinned more, pushing the bread basket in his direction. Logan scowled; he was the leader of their pride, though his brothers still felt the urge to ridicule him. Their family might be only five brothers, but it would expand soon. It had to expand soon. They all needed mates, lionesses to hunt with them, to give them cubs. He'd given up on finding his true mate, the other half of his soul, and was prepared to settle for someone he could live with long enough to fill his home with children.

"There are options, some of them more appealing than others." He poured more wine for himself, ignoring Carter's raised glass and chocolate-smeared face. "A matchmaking service, online dating, the bars, social clubs, the auction."

The auction. Edgar's expression hardened. "No."

Logan didn't blink. "We explore all options. Including that one, if need be."

The others grew restless. No one like the idea of the auction, but most shifters had at least considered participating. Some parts of the country and some types of shifters produced more females than others. Female shifters, regardless of species, were strong enough to mate with other shifters, which was not always the case with pure humans. So those shifters occasionally got together to offer an auction of their eligible women. Everyone assured the purchasers that the women went willingly to the auction, although there were rumors that wasn't always the case.

As much as his stomach turned to think of purchasing an unwilling woman, the idea of his kind becoming extinct nearly stopped his heart. The lions were on the verge of disappearing. He was the alpha of one of the last prides in the country. If they went — the rest of the prides would not be far behind.

Atticus, the youngest, frowned as he played with a coffee spoon still on the pristine white tablecloth, the utensil doll-small in his massive hand. "Isn't there a matchmaker for the wolves? Maybe we could hire them."

"That's a possibility." Logan glanced at Edgar, his second in command. "Look into it, make contact with someone if need be and establish price and timeline."

Benedict, the middle son and the clown, studied him for a long time before speaking. "Why the sudden motivation to get this sorted? We've been wandering around for a couple of decades without much urgency, but now we're all going to find mates in a month? Why?"

Logan pinched the bridge of his nose. The chef's face flooded his vision for no reason, her smooth pale skin with a smattering of freckles across her nose only making those blue eyes snap. And those lips — full and sensuous, as if she were someone who enjoyed the hell out of every kind of sin. He shook himself, ignoring the others' smiles. "Another pride broke up. Their last female died, the cub died with her. That means there are exactly three lionesses left, only one of age to bear cubs."

Silence.

Logan sighed, rubbing the back of his neck. He wanted out of that damn suit, but they'd gone straight from work to dinner. Sitting in a boardroom beat fighting on the savannah, but not by much. He'd rather spend his days in nature; too bad there wasn't any money in it. The expensive watch gleamed from his wrist as he checked the time. "So, gentlemen, this is serious business. That does not mean run out and knock up the first girl you take home, but we need to be deliberate in our choices and our focus. We'll start with the matchmakers and leave the auction as the absolute last resort. There's one in three months, from what the wolves said, so if we do not have at least one of us with a mate, we'll go there. No argument."

It would come later. He knew just by looking at Edgar's face.

Before any of them could speak, the waiter returned to ask for any additional requests or orders, and then provided the bill. Logan gritted his teeth and deliberately ignored the kid. Edgar glanced at the bill, about to hand it over with the corporate credit card, but paused to take a closer look. He looked at the waiter. "The steaks aren't on here."

The kid's expression didn't change, and Logan had to grudgingly admit he was very professional. Well-trained, certainly. "Chef said not to charge for the returned meals."

Benedict, ever the prankster, winked at the kid. "That wasn't really what she said, was it."

The waiter looked on the verge of smiling. "Not — exactly, sir."

Logan wanted to punch his brother as Benedict went on, practically elbowing Atticus in his glee. "Come on, what did she really say?"

"She may have said the bum who lives in the alley traded two hours of washing dishes for both steaks, and she considered that fair payment. He did not get the risotto."

All said with a reasonably straight face.

Edgar handed over the credit card. "She'd rather feed the homeless dude who can't pay than a customer who would? Doesn't seem like a good business decision."

"She always feeds the homeless, sir." The waiter took the card, back to expressionless. "She stays late to prepare the leftovers for them."

And that left Logan feeling like more of a jackass.

But necessity was the mother of invention, after all, and as they waited for the server to return, the seeds of a plan worked into his brain. He couldn't get the chef out of his mind. He didn't even know her name, just the way her accent got stronger as she yelled at him and actually stomped her foot in anger. He stared at the swinging door to the kitchen, his superior hearing catching a thread of her laughing voice. No telling what it meant.

His chest tightened as she passed by the window in the door and a curl of chestnut hair caught his attention. Beautiful. Almost too classically feminine for someone that feisty.

"Logan."

He shook off the spell she cast over him and frowned at Edgar. "Yeah."

"You ready, or going to take a run at the kitchen?" The solemn security chief only raised an eyebrow, though Benedict came perilously close to giggling.

"Let's go." As he stood, Logan pulled out his wallet and dropped a stack of cash on the table.

Edgar cleared his throat. "I already —"

"I pay for my meals. Even if they're sent back." Logan turned and strode out of the restaurant, the chef's musical laugh chasing him out the door. He pulled out his phone and dialed his realtor. There were plans to set in motion.

chapter 2

Two days later as I stalked the delivery entrance of the restaurant before dawn, the owner called. I juggled the largest cup of coffee I could carry and my cell phone, barking orders as the vegetable guy tried to unload some dicey-looking kale. I managed to answer the phone without scalding myself. "Hey, Bob. What's up?"

"Morning, Natalia. Everything's fine. We got an unusual request yesterday."

"Oh?" I frowned as I gestured at the vegetable guy and aimed a kick at the crate of bruised eggplant he carried past, mouthing 'Are you fucking kidding me?' when he feigned surprise. Dick.

"Yes. Apparently a guest was so impressed with your food he requested you prepare a private meal at his home, for his family."

I snorted, setting my coffee down so I could dig through the bags of onions they unloaded. Organic, locally-sourced produce my ass. "I don't think that's going to happen."

"He offered to compensate the restaurant your full salary for the evening, to pay for a replacement chef, and pay you an additional ten thousand dollars."

The onions landed with a splat on the muddy ground, my phone almost following. "How much?"

"Exactly." Bob chuckled. "He apparently really loved your risotto. And the soufflé. He asked specifically about the soufflé. So. Tonight."

"Tonight?" I turned in a circle, searching for something or someone. Certain it was a dream. Ten grand would go a long way toward paying the bills and rent and helping out at the soup kitchen. "I don't know if I can get a replacement. It's such short notice —"

"Apparently it's a special occasion." Bob cleared his throat. "This is important, Nat. He's well-connected, CEO of some big corporation here in the city. This would open doors for us."

I rubbed my forehead, no longer paying attention to anyone else on the loading dock. My mind raced to think of someone who could run the kitchen for me. Jake could be trusted with my menu. "Okay. I'll see if I can get someone. We'll figure it out."

"Good." Bob gave me details for the guy's secretary, who apparently had the requested menu as well as directions.

By the time I'd scribbled the phone number on the back of my hand and hung up, the vegetable guy was gone, but his crates of sub-par produce remained. Irritated, I started making calls for a new vegetable guy and carried my coffee inside the restaurant to plan without freezing to death.

I hadn't found the vegetable guy but managed to recover my equilibrium ten hours later by the time I drove up to a massive wrought-iron gate of what could only be described as a compound outside the city at six o'clock that night. The speaker box crackled before I could ring the bell, and a disembodied voice said, "Ms. Spencer, please drive up to the house. You may park along the west side of the driveway. Someone will meet you."

"Uh, okay," I said, but it was lost in the static and the rumble of the opening gates. I may have added, "Holy fucking shit" for my own benefit, but hoped it was also lost in the noise.

My piece of shit car wheezed into the circle drive around a giant fountain in front of a white mansion that had to be at least four stories and half a dozen wings. I drove around to the far side of the circle and parked the car, no idea if that was the west side of the driveway, and unloaded a few bags of groceries.

As I bumped the door closed with my hip, the front door of the mansion opened and a man in a black suit appeared. A butler. A goddamn butler. He smiled with restrained cordiality, inclining his head as he reached for the bags. "Ms. Spencer, please. Let me take those. Is there anything else?"

"Uh, no. That's it." I cleared my throat, absently patting the shoulder bag that contained my chef's coat, apron, and knives. "I can carry those, really, it's not a problem."

"This way, please." He turned on his heel, every movement crisp, and bustled back into the house. I hurried to keep up, almost slipping on the stairs up to the massive wood and iron door. He paused in the foyer to close the door behind me. "May I take your coat, Ms. Spencer?"

"I can hang it up," I said, shedding the coat and scarf and looking for a place to put it.

The butler may have been hiding a smile as he called to someone else in the house, and another man in a suit appeared, whisking away my coat without a word. I scrubbed a hand through my hair and tried not to stare. It looked like a house from the movies or at least a magazine. Marble floor in the foyer and a double curved staircase sweeping from either side of the open room created a sense of classic grandeur that was lacking in most of the McMansions around the city. To the right was an open gallery with a grand piano and a couple of weird little pianos, the walls covered with portraits.

My jaw shut with a click as the butler inclined his head toward the interior of the mansion. "This way, Ms. Spencer."

I followed, clearing my throat. "Forgive me, I didn't ask your name."

"It's Hamilton, miss. I am the senior butler for Mr. Chase and his family."

"Good to — good to meet you, Hamilton."

He led the way through a few twists and turns to what I assumed was the back of the house and an unbelievably enormous kitchen. It easily dwarfed the restaurant's kitchen, with two of everything — massive commercial quality fridges, cooktops, wall ovens, dishwashers. An island in the middle of the kitchen could easily seat ten people around two sides, with a pot filling station on the side nearest the cooktops.

The butler placed the bags on the island, then turned to look at where I'd stopped short in surprise. "Mr. Chase will be down directly to provide specific guidance. They would like to eat at seven thirty. Is there anything I can assist you wish, Ms. Spencer?"

My mouth worked soundlessly for a good ten seconds as I stared at the acres of cupboards and drawers. "Um... Do you have a map I could use to find things?"

That definitely got a smile, quickly hidden. Hamilton cleared his throat and composed himself to seriousness as he opened a drawer in the island and pulled a laminated card from its depths. "We have frequently found a guide useful, Ms. Spencer. Hopefully this will suffice?"

"Thank God," I said under my breath as I took the card. "Otherwise I'd be looking for a spatula until tomorrow."

"If you have any questions, please use this," he said, pointing to a phone on the wall. "It will dial to the main office; they will be able to find me."

"Sounds good." I rubbed my hands together and pulled on my coat. "Would you like anything, Hamilton? I make a mean grilled cheese."

Definitely got a smile that time, and it stuck around as he said, "Thank you, Ms. Spencer, I may take you up on that later. Please call if you have any questions." He gave almost a half-bow as he retreated.

I shook my head, laughing a little as I tied the apron and unrolled my knives. Nice guy. Hopefully the mysterious Mr. Chase was equally nice, or at least not a total douche. I hummed to myself, poking through cupboards and drawers to find what I needed. Steaks and risotto, the house specialty.

Steps echoed on the marble or stone floor and I turned, hoping it was Hamilton back for a grilled cheese. My blood ran cold as the burly man in jeans and t-shirt strode into the kitchen, carrying three bottles of wine.

"You." My throat almost didn't work. But it was him, all right — the corporate raider from the restaurant. All six foot something of him, tanned and muscled and smiling as he set the bottles down on the island. His biceps, hidden by the suit before, were probably the same size as my thighs. Brown eyes, mild as milk chocolate, studied me briefly before he went to retrieve wine glasses from a cupboard near the cooktop.

"Me."

"Wh-what are you doing here?" I pinched myself to get control. I was a grown damn woman. I could not be stuttering like a fool around that man. He was a jerk and would no doubt take any hesitation as weakness. I couldn't afford to show any weakness — even when my knees knocked together at the way the muscles slid under his t-shirt as he uncorked one of the bottles.

"I live here."

My hands braced on my hips, and I flushed as his slow gaze landed there instead of my face. "What the hell is going on?"

He shrugged, something like mischief in his eyes and the corner of his mouth. He filled two glasses with red wine from the old, old bottle and placed it on the island next to me. "I want you to make me dinner. Since I didn't get to enjoy the meal on Monday, this seemed easier than trying to get reservations."

I laughed in disbelief. "Seriously?"

"I'm always serious," he said, leaning to clink his glass against the one next to me before taking a sip. He frowned at the wine, swirling it a little.

My mind didn't want to register the absurdity of the entire situation. He'd paid close to twelve grand, easily, rather than try to get reservations. The first response that escaped was incoherent French, then I managed to get hold of my temper. "This is — ridiculous. I'm not going to cook for you."

"Oh?" His eyebrows rose a touch. "Why not?"

"This —" I shook my head, started to untie my apron as another incredulous laugh snuck out. "I can't encourage this kind of behavior."

He laughed, loud enough I jumped and almost knocked over my wine. The corporate raider rubbed his mouth, still chuckling, and sketched a slight bow. "I promise, this is the only time I've done something like this."

"I don't believe that." I wadded up the apron. "And I don't need the money."

It was only a small lie. Ten thousand dollars would buy a lot of ... everything.

"Maybe." He studied me closely, head tilted. "But you definitely need the job, right?"

"Are you threatening to call my boss?" I drew my shoulders back and clenched my fists. Ready to fight. The bastard might be sexy to the point of my good sense taking a walk, but he wouldn't dazzle me out of my kitchen.

"I'm threatening to fire you," he said.

"How *dare* you, you don't —"

"I bought the restaurant," he told the wine glass with a frown.

My heart sank. "You — what?"

"I bought it." He straightened from his lean against the counter to nudge the wine glass closer to me, and then reached for the groceries. "The owners were happy to sell. We finished the paperwork this afternoon. It helped that I paid twice what it's actually worth. And most of that value was tied to you." He nodded in my direction, as if that were a good thing. "You are a most in-demand chef, Natalia."

The way he said my name, all slow and drawn out, made my hands tingle. As if he tasted every syllable. I sought refuge in anger, though — he threatened to fire me, even knowing I was the only valuable thing about that restaurant. But panic bubbled in my stomach as well. I'd worked hard to make that kitchen and that staff perfect, like family. I couldn't lose that. Except for Joey. He would definitely have to go. Pride was a stupid reason to lose the best gig I'd found.

The silence stretched as I stared at the island, finally reaching for the wine glass with numb fingers. Shit. I managed to shake off the sinking feeling, trying to see him as the new employer instead of an asshole customer with an ass that didn't quit. It should have been illegal for men like him to wear jeans. "What are your plans, then? For the restaurant."

I could have kicked myself for adding the last bit, particularly as he smiled at the bags of food. "First, you're going to cook me and my brothers dinner. Then you and I can talk about the future of the restaurant."

He looked up and fixed me with a penetrating stare, though there was no threat in it. More like he tried to look into my soul, read my past, measure my worth with his eyes alone. My heart beat faster and sweat broke out on my palms.

I swallowed hard as I reached for a kitchen towel. I'd worked with bigger assholes and sexier men — well, maybe not sexier, but definitely as sexy. Re-buttoning my chef's coat provided a convenient distraction from his long, dark lashes and the small white scar on his chin. "Very well. It'll take an hour if you want the risotto."

"I want everything." His voice went husky and goose-bumps spread over my arms. Then Logan smiled, just a hint of white teeth. "Please. Get started."

"I'll call you when it's —"

"I'll watch."

"I beg your pardon?"

"I'm going to watch you cook." He pulled out a stool on the far side of the island and rested his elbows on the smooth quartz top. "Go ahead."

I stared at him for so long I thought he would speak again, but he only waited. Sipped his wine. Watching me with those damn laughing eyes and sexy smile. I gritted my teeth. If I could cook under the disapproving glare of chefs with four Michelin stars, I could grill a damn steak in front of some ridiculous playboy with no taste. I spun on my heel and started sharpening my knives.

chapter 3

From the way she sharpened the knives, Logan was reasonably sure the chef wanted to stick one between his ribs. He didn't blame her. He hadn't meant to purchase the restaurant right out from under her, but the owners weren't interested in selling a controlling share. They wanted to sell the whole damn thing. Apparently they'd been underwater on their loans for some time and were a hot second from shutting the doors entirely. The only thing keeping them open was her — Natalia Spencer, one of the most in demand, up-and-coming chefs in the city and the entire country.

His accountants still worked through the books, as there were some questionable numbers related to the suppliers and the manager, but Logan was committed. The restaurant was his and with it — so was she.

Natalia worked quickly and efficiently, something he appreciated more than he could articulate. Watching her move around the kitchen reminded him of the werepanthers — sleek and silent and deadly, with none of the lumbering gravitas of the lions and tigers. No, she would be a panther. He refilled his glass with the good wine, the stuff he kept in the back of the cellar so Atticus wouldn't glug it down like the box wine he got at the gas station.

Logan caught a clove of garlic as it shot out from under the flat of her knife, and Natalia frowned. He handed it back, made sure his fingers brushed hers as the clove slipped free, and hid a smile at the way she jumped. So the master chef was not impervious to charm. Neither was he, though, as the spark that zinged between them startled him as well.

She wasn't impressed, though, instead shoving a cutting board, an onion, and small knife at him. "Make yourself useful. Small dice, this size." She flashed a pinky nail at him.

The urge to catch her hand, study the petite nail, take her finger in his mouth, nearly overwhelmed him. Instead, he studied the knife. "For ten grand, I have to cut my own onion?"

"If you're in my kitchen, you work."

"And here I thought this was my kitchen."

She gave him a sideways look, then pointed the big knife at him. "Wherever I cook is my kitchen." The blade dipped to indicate the onion. "So if you're going to sit there mooning at me, you work."

He thought about calling Edgar or Benedict, making them do the work so he could just watch her, but he knew better. The moment his brothers intruded, Logan would be the butt of not-so-subtle jokes, and that would spook the girl. The last thing he needed was Benedict asking her to marry into the family, even in jest.

So he started cutting the onion, frowning as it rolled and he couldn't get the rough peel off. He paused as he caught her watching, her expression almost comical in its consternation. As if she hadn't considered for a moment that he wouldn't know how to cut a damn onion. Logan tried to sound dignified. "Yes?"

"I've never seen that — technique."

"I doubt my advanced onion chopping is on the curriculum at Le Cordon Bleu."

She snorted, shaking her head as she pounded the steaks and threw the garlic into a pan with hot oil. The sizzle and mouth-watering aroma of sautéing garlic filled the kitchen. He kept chopping at the damn onion, though none of the pieces came out even or small enough. She leaned her elbows on the island, eyebrow raised as she studied his handiwork.

"Don't say a word," Logan said, irritated but also pleased he'd amused her.

Natalia chewed her lip furiously, but a smile escaped nonetheless. "Right. Of course." She took the cutting board and dumped the onion in with the garlic, shaking her head as she said over her shoulder, "Don't you dare blame those onions on me. My mentors would hunt me down and take away my toque if they thought I served such raggedy food."

"I cannot promise your name won't come up if the onions are an issue." Logan refilled her wine glass. "My brothers will be kind to you, but they will never let me forget it if I fail."

She made a thoughtful noise, absently sipping the wine as she checked a simmering pot of broth. She stirred it with a graceful flourish before searching for something else in the grocery bags.

"What?" Logan just wanted to hear her talk, no matter the subject. He also wanted her to lose that damn bulky white coat. At least a stupid bandanna didn't cover the cascade of wavy hair down her back, though it was pulled away from her face and the food. The delicate line of her shoulder and throat called to him when her coat gapped, distracting him as she turned on the oven and fiddled with the controls.

Natalia bent to glance into the oven and the chef coat lifted enough to show an amazing ass as her jeans stretched. He shifted on the stool, adjusting himself to conceal the effect she had. She had unbelievable curves, soft and inviting in all the right places. He wanted to squeeze her ass and hips, wrap himself around her, bury his face in her breasts. Rip that bulky, unflattering chef contraption off her and find the soft curves underneath.

She was talking, and he had no idea what she said. Logan forced his concentration back to her voice, rather than the bird thin bones of her wrists and the tiny scars that decorated her hands and forearms. "I'm sorry, what was that?"

"I said I did not envision 'brothers' when your secretary said I would cook for your family."

Logan raised an eyebrow. "Oh?"

Her face flushed, from the heat of the oven or something else he couldn't tell. "Yes. With a house this big, I figured there would be a dozen kids running around."

"Mm." He didn't say anything else, frowning down at his wine. He'd expected to have a dozen kids running around, as well. Sometimes fate did not lead down the roads expected.

The silence stretched and she concentrated on the risotto, stirring and stirring and stirring as she ladled broth into the pan, absently rubbing her shoulder though the spoon never paused. Logan wanted to squeeze her shoulders and draw her back against his chest. Smell her hair and skin. Lick the sweat from her cheek as steam rose from the cooking pasta. Press her up against the cabinets until her legs wrapped around his waist.

Natalia didn't look up from the stove, her words almost lost in the steam and bubbles. "Why are you staring at me?"

"Why do you think I'm staring at you?"

She sighed and tapped the enormous aluminum stockpot on the rear burner. "Shiny metal surface acts as a mirror, genius."

"You shouldn't talk to your boss like that."

"A boss shouldn't stare at my ass like that, either, so I guess we're both in the wrong."

He snorted, ducking his head. Drummed his fingers on the island as he debated how much to say without spooking her. Finally, he settled for something close to the truth.

"No one has ever yelled at me like you did. Ever. It... surprised me. You surprised me. I wanted to learn more about you, and I wanted to finally eat a damn steak."

Natalia made a thoughtful noise, her shoulders tense as she moved the heavy pan off the heat and reached for a pile of freshly grated cheese. "Is that why you bought the restaurant?"

"Not entirely." But mostly.

She checked the steaks, still warm and raw on the cutting board, and his mouth watered. The beef smelled amazing — fresh and fatty and tender, minimally processed without antibiotics or hormones or any of the shit that most meat seemed to be steeped in. His lion wanted to eat it raw, tear into it with teeth and hands until the blood coated his tongue with iron. After a very long pause, Natalia glanced at him from under her gorgeous, dark eyelashes, her expression unfathomable. "You should talk to Joey. The manager."

Logan leaned forward. "Why is that?"

"I'm just the chef," she said. She checked the heat in a fresh skillet, frowning at the burner and adjusting the flame before re-checking. Natalia picked up the steaks and settled them in the pan. "I don't know what goes on in the back office. But he does a lot of business that has nothing to do with food, it seems."

He looked at his phone, sent a quick message to the accountants: *Look at the manager*. Then he returned his attention to his chef and the delicious handfuls of her ass that begged to be squeezed. "I'll look into it. Thank you. And, out of curiosity — what happened to the accent?"

"I'm only French when I'm angry," she said, a hint of smile creating a dimple in her cheek. "Bad habit from school — the boys couldn't understand if I cursed at them in an American accent, so I started faking a French accent so they could understand."

"It's very ... intriguing." Logan smiled to himself as she flushed and turned back to the stove, and inhaled the scent of her.

"Against my better judgment," she said suddenly, waving tongs over her shoulder at him. "I will give you a steak I would never serve to a real customer. But I assume your brothers have more discerning palates?"

"Not very discerning." He glanced over his shoulder at where the four lions waited in the dining room. Hopefully on their best behavior. "Prepare their steaks however you like."

She muttered under her breath in what he thought was French. Logan went to the intercom and called the front office, "Send Karen up to serve dinner, will you? Thanks." He refilled both of their wine glasses. He watched her finish the steaks and plate them, deliberate in her preparation of six meals. Asparagus and sautéed kale completed the dinner. "We have a young lady who will serve the meal. I am sure my brothers would like to meet you."

Natalia flushed, still fussing with onc of the plates. "It's fine, I'll just —"

"Come on," he said, carrying her wine. She followed reluctantly, and he held the door to the dining room open. "Gentlemen, I believe you remember Ms. Natalia Spencer?"

A chorus of raucous cheering nearly knocked her back a step, and the chef blinked. Logan shook his head, pulling out a chair for her to the left of his seat at the head of the table. She cleared her throat, a little wide-eyed. "Uh, hi."

Edgar nodded, "Ms. Spencer, welcome. Please, have a seat."

She blinked, looking around. "No, thank you. I couldn't possibly. I have to prepare the soufflé —"

"Eat with us," Benedict said, winking roguishly, and she blushed. The middle son was not as burly or intimidating as the others, and certainly only half the size of youngest brother Atticus. But he'd had enough success with women that Logan made a note to talk to him about flirting with Natalia. There would be none of that. "Please."

It took her a moment to fully grasp the set-up, counting the people and the place settings before saying, "There are only five of you."

"Yes," Logan said.

"You told me to prepare six steaks."

"Yes."

She frowned at him. "And the sixth is for ...?"

"You." He pulled her chair out a little farther, nodding at it. "Since it would not be right to have you do all the work and not enjoy the outcome."

She didn't look convinced. "Do you always ask the help to eat with you?"

For a moment he didn't know what to say. They never asked anyone to join family dinner, even their business partners. Family dinner was only for family, no one else. She would never know the honor shown her that night, and part of him mourned that he might never be able to fully explain. Unless she understood the lion and shifter parts of their lives, she wouldn't understand the role of food and meals and bonding. Logan managed a smile. "You're not 'the help,' Natalia, but no, we don't ask many people to eat dinner with us."

"Just special people," Carter said under his breath, a little shy.

Her attention snapped to him, and Logan's hackles rose protectively for his younger brother. Carter had a good heart but wasn't expert at reading social situations. He often mis-spoke and had been teased relentlessly at school for being a little different, a little out-there. He had an artist's heart, their mother used to say. A dreamer's soul.

Logan held his breath, wondering if the chef would react as sharply to the younger man as she would have to him, but instead, Natalia's expression softened. She attempted a smile, if a wobbly, uneasy one, and patted Carter's shoulder. "Thank you. I'll sit for a moment, but then I have to prepare dessert."

He knew at that moment that she was right for their family. She was perfect. She read Carter, understood his dreamer's soul, and didn't chastise him. Didn't expect him to be something he wasn't, and didn't make the boy feel bad about it, either. Logan's chest tightened, and his lion started to rumble. The lion wanted to mark her immediately so none of the other shifters in the city would dare look at her sideways. He forced himself to calm as he eased her chair into the table, then took his own just to her right. As soon as the others followed suit, Karen and another butler swept into the dining room with the first round of plates.

Logan added a touch more wine to her glass, sitting back as his brothers steamrolled into both the meal and the chef. Benedict, the lawyer, started asking detailed questions about the restaurant's debts and relationship to a soup kitchen a few blocks away, an odd note that had been highlighted in the contract and transfer of ownership.

She flushed, looking away before answering. "That was my — condition. For working at the restaurant. They had to run or at least support a soup kitchen. Bob and his wife couldn't afford to run their own, but we found the soup kitchen close by, so that was good enough."

Edgar, already halfway through his steak and making indecent noises as he chewed, paused to breathe. "Why a soup kitchen?"

Again, her gaze slid away. One shoulder shrugged and she concentrated on her plate. "I know what it's like to be hungry."

When Edgar opened his mouth to ask a follow-up, Logan shook his head. Off-limits. So his second-in-command changed topics, poking at the asparagus. "Are there cameras outside the restaurant? The loading dock area? It's a dark alley, with a blind spot, and the doors aren't very secure. I'm surprised they haven't been robbed."

"They were." She leaned back in her chair, holding the wine glass as if it were an extension of her arm. "Three months ago. Someone ripped off most of our appliances, cookware, a couple of computers. All the good stuff was gone, so we're making do with thrift store replacements."

Logan raised his eyebrows and looked at Benedict, who shook his head.

Natalia pinched the bridge of her nose. "They didn't report it, did they?"

"No." Logan took a deep breath, putting that headache off until he could get into the office the next morning and call those owners, his realtor, and his accountants. Someone would explain what the hell was going on with this restaurant. And that manager as well. He wanted to enjoy his first meal with Natalia, watch her eat knowing he provided food for her and she was safe, warm, protected by his family. "But that can wait. Does the soup kitchen know it is named as part of this contract?"

"I doubt it." She picked at the risotto and steak, only partially through the meal despite that his brothers had already licked their plates clean. "They just know I show up on Wednesdays and Saturdays with produce and bread and soup and sometimes other things."

"And you feed the homeless that gather in the alley behind the restaurant as well," Edgar added.

Natalia looked up sharply. "How did you —"

He smiled down at his plate, waving a hand. "Not important. But I will keep it in mind when we increase the security."

Logan relaxed as the conversation veered into something less interesting, less focused on Natalia, and his brothers argued over some football game. His hand rested on the table near hers, close enough to touch but not quite there. She smiled a few times at the ridiculousness of his brothers, but there was kindness in her when she looked at Carter. When she slid her chair back from the table, they all rose as well, and she froze, still bent over. Logan folded his napkin and helped with her chair. "The ladies' room is —"

"No," she said, a hint of a flush pinking her cheeks. "I need to finish the soufflé. For dessert."

Logan nodded, then glanced at his brothers. "Perhaps Carter can help you?"

His brother jumped at the chance, talking a mile a minute as he walked Natalia back to the kitchen. Logan waited until the servers removed their plates before addressing the other three men. "Something's going on at the restaurant, something to do with the manager. I don't want any of it blowing back on her. Understood?"

Edgar leaned back in his chair, frowning up at the ceiling and overly-elaborate chandelier. "I'll look into it tomorrow. If we need to send a message, Atticus can deliver it." He eyed their youngest but scariest brother.

Atticus grunted as he tore into his fourth or fifth dinner roll. "Just let me know whose legs need breaking."

"Good." Logan stared unseeing at the chair she'd vacated, right next to him. Missing her already.

"So she's it, huh?"

He frowned up at Benedict. "What?"

"She's who you've been searching for." Benedict was, for once, entirely serious. "You know?"

"She doesn't know anything about us." Logan sighed, wiped his mouth and fiddled with his dessert fork. "I can't expect her to reciprocate when she doesn't — she doesn't feel as deeply as we do, as quickly. She might be interested in being a girlfriend, but I doubt she's ready to be a mate. It will take time."

Edgar looked thoughtful more than anything. "Maybe not as long as you think, Logan. She likes you. Just be honest."

He glanced at his phone as the accountant called, and got up from the table. "I'll be back. If you touch my soufflé, I'll rip out your fucking throats."

His thoughts remained on Natalia as he spoke to the accountant about the cooked books at the restaurant, and part of his heart warmed as Edgar's words settled close. She liked him.

chapter 4

The soufflé was a big hit. It disappeared almost as quickly as the steaks had — I blinked, and there were only traces of chocolate in the ramekins, on their faces, on the spoons they licked clean. I managed to hide a smile but just barely; cooking for hungry men was usually rewarding work. And every part of me felt electrified from where Logan touched my hand when he pulled out my chair for the second time. Heat surged to my cheeks every time he moved and his clothes rustled, or his chair squeaked, or he sipped wine like he could taste me. My heart jumped to my throat and I tried to remember my professionalism. I was an employee, regardless of how hard he stared at my ass when I walked back to the kitchen. Just an employee. It became a mantra as I scrubbed the pans and my knives, not looking at him though I knew he followed me out of the dining room and took up his stance leaning against the island.

"I'll give you free rein with the restaurant," he said abruptly, and I dropped the risotto pan into a sink full of water.

I faced him, soaked. "What?"

Half his mouth curled in a smile as he handed me a dry towel. "You set the menu, the prices, hire and fire the staff, whatever. On one condition."

Hope rose in my heart as I patted my face dry. I could run the restaurant, nip all that corrupt shit in the bud and finally serve what *I* wanted to serve. No more catering to uninformed dilettantes. We could streamline donations, maybe set up a mobile food truck to go around to the homeless shelters. "What's the — what condition?"

He shrugged, brown eyes sparking with amusement and something else I couldn't quite identify. "Every now and then, you cook for us. For me. If I call, you come here."

My hands dropped to my sides and I deflated. The dream wisped away. Running at his beck and call was off-putting enough, but the thought of constantly being around him, those damn sexy eyes and the enormous hands that gripped the counter as if he could break off a chunk of quartz with only a little effort... My self-control wasn't strong enough to protect me from him, even that husky rumbly voice he had. *Especially* from that husky rumbly voice, so damn close to a purr I wanted to let him wrap himself around my legs. I shook myself out of it. "I appreciate the offer, but I can't. I'll stick around until you can find —"

"Wait." He straightened, took a stalking step towards me, and I jumped back out of instinct, jamming my back into the edge of the counter. He stopped short, expression unreadable. I flushed. At length, Logan went on, voice quiet and controlled. "You'd give up full creative and management control of the restaurant just so you won't have to cook for me? What the hell is wrong with you?"

Luckily, the damp towel and my still-dripping coat gave me a reason to look away from him, to convince myself what I said was true, and it was about the food rather than him. And his jeans. And maybe the t-shirt that stretched across the chest of a Greek god. "I don't like preparing bad food. And you — your taste is terrible. That's the worst steak I've ever served and it is a — professional embarrassment that I put it in front of you."

At least partially true, though the 'yummy' noises he made were gratifying enough. Even if they made me wonder if those were his sex noises, too. My cheeks caught fire and his head tilted as he studied me, as if he couldn't figure out why I blushed.

I bit my lip and turned away, shedding the chef's coat to toss over one of the stools to dry. At least the thin sweater I wore remained dry, though it clung more than I remembered. A strangled noise had me look back, and I froze; Logan looked as though he wanted to kiss me. His gaze lingered on my waist and breasts, more defined in the much smaller sweater, and after a long time, he looked at my lips. I held my breath.

"How about —" He cut off, cleared his throat. "When I want you to cook for me, you will choose the menu, and I will eat what you prepare. I may suggest a cuisine or general region — Italian or French, maybe. Will that suffice?"

It felt like a trap. Like too much remained unsaid. There had to be some other motivation.

I concentrated on drying my knives and putting them away. When nothing remained to distract me from him, I put my hands on my hips. "Why did you buy the restaurant?"

"Because I felt like it."

When I looked at him in silence, refusing to accept such a blithe answer, he laughed. Logan raised his hands in surrender. "I swear. You made me so mad I called my realtor and told him to make an offer on the restaurant. By the time I calmed down — well, by the time Edgar talked sense into me, we'd already made the offer and I didn't want to back out."

"You can't be serious." I rolled up my knives and shoved them into my shoulder bag. "No one spends *that* much money just because they're mad."

He shrugged. "I have a lot of money."

I shook my head and continued packing my things. It felt like lies, though I couldn't pinpoint exactly what made me uneasy. By the looks of his house, he could buy whatever he wanted, including my restaurant. But he didn't look like the kind of man who made rash judgments, and I doubted very much he accumulated that much money by making stupid investment decisions. I massaged my temples as I faced him, trying to read the truth in his eyes without letting the defined muscles in his forearms distract me. "Restaurants are notorious money pits. Most fail in the first year. We're barely six months old. Why take the risk?"

His fingers drummed an even tattoo on the counter. He finally pointed at one of the stools at the island. "Sit, please." He waited until I perched on the stool before going on. "First, the real estate itself is valuable. You're on a trendy street, and if I wanted to get rid of the restaurant and put in a coffee shop or hip clothing store, I could and I would be able to recoup any losses. So that's a sound investment. Second, it took me two weeks to get a reservation. It doesn't take me more than two hours to get a reservation anywhere in this city."

When I snorted, he held up his phone, eyebrows raised in challenge. "Give me a restaurant, and I'll get a reservation right now. We can go get coffee."

I put a hand to my forehead, flabbergasted.

Logan put the phone on the island, still watching me. "So I knew the restaurant had a unique product, something that was worth that type of wait. Something that added immense value to the venue as it existed when I went in there. You."

"That's ridiculous, don't —"

"I'm not blowing smoke at you, darlin, it's the God's honest truth." He stumbled over 'darlin,' and so did my heart. Logan plowed on, though, as if neither of us heard it or the purr in his voice. "And third, the food was good. More than good. What I got to taste of it." He gave me a sideways look that made my skin prickle in anticipation. "So from where I sat, it wasn't much of a risk."

“Bob could barely pay his loans,” I said, slow and careful so he wouldn’t misunderstand. “I couldn’t get the good suppliers because we never paid on time. Three weeks ago, they turned off the lights for four hours until Joey came up with the money to pay the electric bill. If it were so profitable and such a sure thing, why the hell were we losing money every night?”

“Because you kicked out paying customers?”

I scowled and he laughed, then reached for my shoulder. Lightning arced between us and I caught my breath. Every part of me warmed with the rough drag of his calloused fingers down my bicep. I couldn’t breathe. Logan’s voice went soft. “Not really, I promise. There’s something else going on, like you said. I’ll figure it out, don’t worry about it. I won’t let it interfere with your work or the soup kitchen. Just cook and run the kitchen for me. Everything else will work out.”

He stood over me, close enough I could have slid my arms around him and pulled him close, could have kissed him if I wanted. He leaned closer, brown eyes searching my face for something, and the breath hiccupped in my throat. Logan touched my cheek. His thumb grazed my lower lip, and my heart started to pound. My brain short-circuited as he eased closer, his palm resting on my waist. His head tilted, lowered.

He wanted to kiss me. The thought filtered sluggish and slow through me as I looked up at him, lips parted in shock or anticipation or just plain necessity. Holy crap on a cracker. Logan smiled very slightly as his mouth descended towards mine, I could feel him smiling more as his lips brushed my temple, my cheek, the corner of my mouth. I jerked away and turned on my heel, panic making my hands shake as I reached for a dry pan. Shit.

Logan cleared his throat. "Natalia —"

"I promised Hamilton a grilled cheese," I said, louder than I intended. The pan clanged against the cooktop but I didn't care, throwing open the fridge to search for cheese and butter and bread and anything so I wouldn't look at him. That giant, capable, unfortunately handsome man who made my lungs contract and my knees wobble. "I told him I'd —"

"Hamilton already ate dinner," Logan said, all slow and careful but with laughter in his voice. As if he knew how unsettled he'd made me. I wondered if that was his game — reduce a confident woman to a puddle of lust and uncertainty and then laugh at her when she couldn't string a thought together.

"Of course." It was easily nine o'clock, maybe later. I didn't dare take out my phone or look around for a clock, lest I peek at him accidentally and trigger whatever spell he'd worked. "I should go."

"Natalia."

God, I loved the way he said my name. Like the Russian way, not the mispronounced version of Natalie I usually heard. Na-tah-lee-uh. I closed my eyes and let it shiver through me. I picked up my wet chef's coat and shoved it in the bag as well, fumbling with my purse as I looked him in the chest. "I'll show myself out. Please give my regards to your brothers."

I fled like a coward and bolted for a door. For any door. After two turns I was hopelessly lost. Logan had trailed after me, far too silent for such a big dude, and at length he said, "This way," gesturing down a different hall.

He walked me to my car and even opened the door for me, waiting as I shoved everything in the backseat. He caught my arm before I could dive into the driver's seat. "You never answered me."

I stared up at him, every inch of me flushed from the feel of his enormous hand wrapped around my elbow. God help me if he tried to kiss me again, I didn't have the strength of will to run away a second time. "Wh-what?"

"About whether you would be my partner."

My jaw went slack. "P-partner?"

"At the restaurant." His smile grew to a grin, and my stomach wobbled and swerved to drop to my feet.

"Oh." I turned and pulled my arm free, ducking into the piece of shit sedan and pulling the door closed. Desperate for some space. I turned the key and prayed it would start; if the engine didn't turn over, he would invite me to wait inside and then I would kiss him. I just knew it. And if I kissed him, it was a very short walk to his bedroom and losing whatever integrity and dignity I had left.

Luckily — or unluckily — the engine chugged to life. I cranked the window down enough to say, "I'll give it a trial run. One month. Okay?"

"I want longer than that," he said. The skin around his eyes creased as he smiled. "But we can start with one month. Drive safely, Natalia."

I want longer than that. It kept repeating in my head, over and over, as I drove back to the city. As I parked the car at my favorite pub and went inside, hoping my best friend would be there. She was, thank God, standing behind the bar with her brother. I snagged a stool near the end of the bar, resting my elbows on the smooth wooden surface, and immediately covered my face with my hands.

Ruby laughed at me, sliding a gin and tonic into my line of vision. "What happened? Jake was in here looking for you. Said you had some kind of gig?"

"Oh my God." I collapsed against the bar and hid my face against my folded arms. "Ruby, you have got to help me."

She nudged me. "Sit up, chica." She squinted at me a little. "What's up?"

We'd met years ago when she tended bar at the only restaurant open late enough to feed the hungry cooks after the other kitchens closed. Now I had my own restaurant, and she and her brother, Rafe, owned their own bar just down the street from it. Her dark hair was cut in a super feminine bob, but everything else about her was tough as nails — the spike through her septum, the tattoos across her chest and arms, piercings up and down her ears, and the bold makeup around her eyes. She also wore steel-toed shit-kickers for when the bar patrons got a little too froggy.

I pinched the bridge of my nose and struggled for calm. "The gig tonight was some super rich dude. I kicked him out of the restaurant a couple days ago because he sent back his steak. Well, he paid Bob off to have me cook at his house and then tells me that he bought the restaurant. He *bought* it, Ruby. Because he was mad."

"Did he fire you?"

"No," I said, still a little incredulous. I drank half the gin and tonic and knew I would regret it the next morning, particularly after having put a dent in Logan's no doubt expensive wine collection. "He wants me to run everything. Set the menu, manage the staff. Everything."

Ruby glanced at her brother, who was eavesdropping rather than pulling beers for the handful of customers hanging out on a weekday night, then back at me. "So what's the problem? That sounds like a solid deal, as long as he's not some creep."

"That's the worst part." I sighed, shaking my head at the glass of gin. "He's not. He's a dick, but he's gorgeous. With a capital 'g.'"

Ruby laughed. "That doesn't sound like the worst part."

I groaned and slapped a hand over my eyes. "He almost kissed me. And I panicked. I ran."

"What are you, twelve?" She bumped my elbow. "You'll be fine. Just suck it up and keep your knives on you. Play hard to get."

"That's terrible advice. You should be —" I half-turned as the door to the bar opened and the bell jingled, distracting me from my own embarrassment. Until I saw the man who walked through — the giant bruiser who was Logan's youngest brother. Atticus. I swore under my breath, about to say something as I turned back to look at my best friend, but Ruby frowned at him as well.

She glanced at Rafe and he made eye contact with Atticus, gesturing for him to come around the bar. The two men disappeared into the back, and I looked at Ruby. "How do you know Atticus?"

She dropped the glass she held, jumping back as it shattered on the floor. She didn't look away from me. "How do *you* know Atticus?"

"He's Logan's little brother. The guy who bought the restaurant — Logan Chase."

Her eyebrows climbed slowly to her hairline. "I'm sorry, what?"

"The capital 'g' gorgeous guy who bought the restaurant," I repeated slowly. My heart sank, though, since the expression on her face did not inspire much confidence. "Was Logan Chase. Atticus is his little brother. Do you think he followed me here?"

Ruby took a breath, looking at where Rafe and Atticus disappeared, then shook her head. Offered a fake smile. "Doubt it. He and Rafe go way back. I wouldn't even worry about it." She fussed with the broom and dustpan, cleaning up the mess before she went on. "You should be careful around the Chase brothers, Nat. Especially Logan."

I braced my hands on the bar as I watched her. Exactly what I needed to know but the last thing I wanted to hear. "Why?"

"Just — be careful. They're used to getting what they want, and they don't always have good brakes. Sometimes people get hurt. It just comes with the territory of having that much power, I guess. Eventually, everything is a commodity to be purchased. Guard your heart, okay?"

"It's nothing," I said, heart sinking. Her words, at least, rang true. Truer than Logan's. "Just a silly crush. I'll be fine. And thanks for the warning."

"Sure." She focused on new glasses but slid me a side look. "But if you get the chance to fuck him, no strings attached, do it. Don't even hesitate."

I laughed, let the gin warm the dread from my stomach, and rested my head on my fist. "Noted. Anyway. What else was going on?"

She filled me in on her day, though she kept looking back at where Rafe and Atticus argued in the shadows of their office. I didn't mind, though, since I kept hearing Logan's gruff voice instead of her pixie-high one. *I want longer than that.* I shivered, trying to concentrate, but nothing could keep his face out of my mind. God help me, I was in trouble.

chapter 5

I had enough of a hangover that waking up the next morning at six to meet the seafood supplier was a special kind of hell. Even double-fisting coffee didn't help. The headache beat behind my eyes as I stood on the loading dock and looked at the crates of fish. I counted them up and made notes on my clipboard. I needed to design the menu for the next week, and there was no telling what Joey would decide to get rid of next. I could try to put salmon on special, change things up a bit.

The greasy-looking guy, smelling very strongly of old bait, held out the invoice for my inspection. "Just what you ordered. Joey was supposed to be here for this delivery, though. Where's he at?"

"I'm not his keeper," I said under my breath, then nudged a crate with my foot. "Some of that mahi mahi looks kinda sweaty. How old is it?"

"Caught it myself this morning, sugar." He lit up a cigarette, waving it at me. "Just sign the papers and get back in the kitchen."

I scowled. "You can go fuck yourself. Take back the mahi mahi, I don't want it."

"Joey wants it," he said, then turned and walked away. His truck started up and drove off before I could open my mouth to yell at him, and I stared at the invoice in my hand.

Unbelievable.

The kid I had helping me in the kitchen in the mornings hauled the rest of the crates into the cooler, though I had him leave the offending mahi mahi on the loading dock. It looked off-color when I examined it more closely, and I started unpacking it. Maybe only the top couple of fish were bad, the others...

I sat back on my heels. Wrapped in cellophane, under two overripe fish, were stacks of cash. Hundreds. Tens of thousands of dollars worth of cash. My breath caught as I touched it, looking around to see if anyone else noticed. Nothing. I was alone in the alley, and suddenly more terrified than any other time I'd been almost alone at the restaurant. Especially with Edgar's comment about no cameras. I swallowed hard, then pulled out my phone. I didn't know what to do about cash in the fish, but there was someone who would.

The phone rang at least six times before he picked up, and he sounded half-asleep, voice all rusty and gruff. "Good morning, Natalia."

Shivers ran all the way through me, sparking heat and fire low in my stomach. Logan sounded like rumpled sheets and soft pillows and tangled limbs. I cleared my throat, glad he couldn't see me blush. "I'm sorry to call so early, but —"

"Not a problem." A rush of breath, as if he yawned, then rustling and movement. "What can I do for you?"

For a moment I thought about answering honestly — or at least correcting his question to 'what can I do *to* you.' I put a hand to my forehead and turned away, praying for maturity and calm. "There's a problem. At the restaurant."

"Oh?" Less flirting, more serious. "What kind of problem? Are you safe?"

"Safe? Yeah, it's just — I got the fish delivery today, and something's wrong with it."

"I don't think I'm the kind of restaurant owner who is overly concerned about —"

"There's money. In the fish." I looked at the mahi mahi, wrinkled my nose. Christ, it smelled.

A long pause. A hint of disbelief in his voice, as if he thought I prank-called at six in the morning. "I'm sorry, say that again?"

I lowered my voice. "There are three crates of mahi mahi, but there are only about six fish in each. Underneath the fish are bundles of cash. Of hundreds. Tens of thousands of dollars. Joey was supposed to be here to accept the delivery, but I haven't seen him all morning, and —"

"Go inside the restaurant." Logan sounded like he was moving very fast, all business and tense. "Lock yourself in one of the offices. Leave the money in the fish, leave the crates where they are. Edgar and Atticus are closer; they should be there in a few minutes. I'm on my way."

"Logan, it's not —"

"Someone put that money there for a reason," he said, his tone that weird overly-calm one used by professionals when the normal people flipped out. Like how doctors talked to incoherent patients. My heart started to beat faster; he was worried. He went on despite the rumble of a car engine in the background, still managing to sound unruffled. "Joey expects it to be there, and since we don't know who put the money there, I don't want you anywhere near that fish. I can't think of many legitimate reasons to put thousands of dollars in fish, can you?"

I backed toward the restaurant, my attention still on the crates. "No, I don't think so."

"Right. Lock yourself in one of the offices, just to be safe in case someone shows up to retrieve the cash, and wait until Edgar or I call you. Okay?"

"S-sure." I cleared my throat, suddenly wishing I had my knives on me. Or a gun. A gun might have been better.

"I'll be there soon. Everything will be fine." It sounded like he wanted to convince himself as much as me.

I concentrated on breathing, "Yeah, it's —" and retreated another step. I bumped into something and froze. Hands grabbed my arms and Joey said, "Going somewhere?" right in my ear.

The phone slipped from my hand and I elbowed him, tried to throw off his grip. Instead, his fingers tightened on my elbow, and he yanked me into the shadows near the edge of the loading dock. "Who were you talking to, Nat?"

"No one." I cleared my throat. "Let me go, Joey. I need to figure out what we're going to do with the salmon this week, and the menus go to the printer in a couple hours."

"You don't want to use the mahi mahi?"

"No." I swallowed, wrenching at his grip once more as I waved at the three crates. "It's shit. Smells off. Send it back."

"Stop fucking around," he said, low and cold. Shoved me up against the wall and pinned me, his forearm a bar across my throat. For a short guy, his upper body strength surpassed mine, even as I kicked at him. "Who did you tell about the money?"

"I don't know what you're talking about," I said. I choked, clawing at his arm and his face. "Let me go."

"You've been a pain in my ass for too long." Joey glanced behind him before looking back at me, exerting more pressure on my throat until my breath rasped. "How about a little lesson in remembering your place, hmm?"

His knee pressed between my thighs, and I screamed. Screamed and prayed someone would hear, would intervene. Joey back-handed me, grabbed my shoulders and slammed me against the wall until my head bounced off the bricks. I swung at him, stomped at his feet, elbowed and raged. Never again. Wasn't going to be a victim again. I clawed at his eyes and he cursed, struggled to keep a hand on me as I fumbled at a loose brick.

I almost had it in hand when he tripped me and I landed hard on my knees, crying out. He landed on top of me, a knee in my back. The frozen concrete burned against my skin as my sweater and coat hiked up, and Joey shoved my cheek to the dirty ground. I tried to breathe. Had to stay calm. Panic meant dead.

His voice hissed in my ear, hateful and cruel. "Should I fuck you out here in the garbage, Nat? Or drag you inside and have you in the cooler? You're a cold fish anyway, might as well —"

The brick in his face cut him off. My shoulder and back screamed as I swung it behind me, into his nose until the blood gushed and spattered across my coat and hair. I shoved at him to get free, desperate to get back on my feet, and screamed again, mostly in rage.

Son of a bitch. That unbelievable, dirty son of a bitch. I elbowed him in the throat, half blind from dirt and his blood.

His fingers dug into my thigh. "Don't you —"

His hand disappeared and then so did the rest of him.

Silence.

I scrambled to my feet, staggering to lean against the brick wall as my knees objected and my back spasmed. Pain everywhere, blinding pain — but escape was more important. Pain would heal. What he threatened — would not. Breath sobbed in my throat as I searched the alley. Ten feet away, a mountain of muscle held Joey by the throat, his heels dangling three feet off the ground. Atticus. He looked at me, unmindful as the much smaller man flopped around in his grip like a dying fish. "Are you okay?"

Was I okay. My mouth opened, I wanted to answer him, but nothing came out. Nothing worked. I inhaled, gulped air, couldn't stop gulping until I choked. Hyperventilated. Stared at him, at Joey, at Edgar, wearing a long dark overcoat and talking into his phone as he approached me.

His voice was calm, soothing as if he spoke to a wild animal. "You're okay, Natalia. We're here. We've got him. Just slow down a little. In through your nose, out through your mouth. Breathe with me, okay? Just like me. In. And out."

He took exaggerated breaths, taking another step closer, and I flinched. Edgar stopped, retreated. Sat on his heels, making himself smaller, less threatening. Tears burned my eyes and I looked away. Great. Just fucking wonderful. Nothing even happened and I was ready to break. I was stronger this time. I wasn't a kid. Joey couldn't hurt me. I stood on my own.

And still I couldn't breathe, couldn't calm anything down as my heart raced and sweat broke out all over me and my stomach heaved at the smell of myself. I stank like bad fish and week-old garbage and old blood, and almost every part of me was sticky. The tears started to fall and I cursed more, turning away to hide my face and the rest of me. God damn it.

chapter 6

Logan felt her scream even when he was still half a mile away. He abandoned the car and ran on foot, cutting through side streets until he burst into the alley behind the restaurant. His heart stopped.

Atticus had a man pinned against the brick wall of the alley, the human's face purple, but his attention was deeper in the alley, near the loading dock. Where Natalia cowered, on her feet but just barely, covered in mud and — blood. Blood.

His vision went red, and a roar tore from his throat in sheer rage. Atticus flinched, started, "Don't scare her —" but Logan couldn't hear.

Edgar lurched to his feet and blocked Logan from immediately grabbing the girl. His security chief walked him back a few steps, though Edgar's shoulders strained with the effort of controlling Logan with the lion in charge. Edgar talked fast and low, trying to get his attention. "She's terrified. Stop making so much fucking noise. We got here in time. He roughed her up a little but nothing — more. Atticus and I will take care of him as soon as we figure out whose money this is. You need to stop being the scary thing and start being the kind thing, do you hear me?"

Logan couldn't look away from her. Natalia trembled, her face bloodless under the smears of dirt. Her clothes were ruined, her phone in pieces, and she stared at him with the kind of vacant fear that nearly unmoored his heart. He'd heard the bastard confront her before her phone cut out, knew he hurt her, and Logan couldn't get there to save her. Couldn't help her when she needed him most.

Edgar smacked his cheek. "Are you listening to me?"

Logan blinked, looked at his brother, but couldn't keep the growl out of his voice. "Did you just hit me?"

"*Listen to me.*" Edgar, expression all hard angles and fury, shook Logan enough to get his attention. "She was just assaulted. How you act now will remain between you for the rest of your lives, do you understand me? Be kind. Be quiet. Listen. No sudden moves, no loud noises, no grabbing. Ask permission, you shithead. You follow her goddamn lead, got it?"

Some of the blind rage faded, replaced with pain and anger. The cold kind of anger that meant if the man survived Atticus, he had an eternity of misery at Logan's hands to look forward to. But Logan took a deep breath. Natalia was more important. Far more important. She looked utterly miserable, still crying as she watched him and Edgar. Logan swallowed his fury and promised the lion they would get to check her over, make sure she was unharmed, but only if they could get close enough without scaring her. He managed to nod to Edgar. "I got it. Go help Atticus. Figure out who left the money and set up a meeting. Then deal with that manager. Do we have clean clothes in your car?"

"We have a go bag but the closest shower is your office." Edgar eased his grip on Logan's shoulders, gave him one more warning look before striding to help their younger brother.

Logan concentrated on being calm and still through every part of his mind and body as he approached Natalia. She still hyperventilated, on the verge of passing out, and Logan leaned inside the loading dock to bring out a stool. He got just close enough to slide it next to her, kept his voice quiet, gentle. "Sit down, baby."

She blinked, looking at the stool. Then at him. Then at the stool. She sat, though it was more like her legs simply gave way. Bloody tears rent the knees of her jeans, so maybe they had. Logan controlled the rage that threatened to spill over once more, and instead eased to sit on his heels. Kept his hands loose and ready, afraid fists would alarm her.

"Are you okay?"

Natalia blinked, blue eyes wide and locked on his face like a lifeline. She shook her head 'no.'

His lion paced, wanted to leap at her and cover her with his scent, mark her so no male would ever be stupid enough to touch her or threaten her or even look at her. He couldn't protect her if she didn't live in his house, if she wasn't with him or people he trusted. Logan struggled for control as his nails grew darker and longer, forcing back the shift. "Are you hurt?"

She shook her head again and searched his face for something. He wondered if his features had begun to change, if his nose remained the correct shape and his eyes stayed brown instead of gold. He cleared his throat. "There are clean clothes and a shower at my office. It isn't far from here. You can get cleaned up, and we can talk about our plan. For the restaurant."

And that time he felt a little silly for adding the qualifier, remembering the way her voice tripped when she'd added the same thing only the night before. Logan took a deep breath, held his hand out a little when he was certain everything remained human. "Does that work? I'll bribe you with coffee."

She shivered, hands still shaking as she fumbled with her coat. "I have to make up the menus. They go to the p-printer at two, and —"

"It's okay," he said. Logan tried to smile instead of snarl, keeping his teeth covered just in case. "It's more than okay. Carter will call the printer and explain we had trouble with a delivery."

A weak laugh, but it was watery and streaked with tears. She started to stand and winced, the breath hissing in her teeth. Logan didn't dare move yet, kept his voice low. "Do you need help?"

"My knees," she said, a curse gritted between her teeth. Her eyes closed and her shoulders slumped.

"Let me help you," he murmured. He waited until she nodded to straighten, moving one deliberate step at a time until he stood next to her. And again his lion almost raged free. She smelled like fear and pain and another man, another man's blood and violence. Logan nearly chewed a hole in the inside of his cheek before he managed to say, "I'll carry you to the car, okay?"

He waited for her trembling nod before putting his arm around her shoulders, carefully lifting under her damaged knees to cradle her against his chest. She shivered and shook, and felt as delicate as a bird captured in his hands. He sighed. "I'm so sorry, Natalia. I should have gotten here faster."

She went rigid, and Logan cursed himself. No feeling sorry for himself, not when she was still a mess. He carried her to where Edgar's car idled on the street, doors still open from where his brothers rushed to her aid. He wanted to kiss her, to nuzzle in her hair until she carried his scent, but instead he said, "Front seat or back seat?"

"I want to go home," she whispered, arms tight around his neck. "Please."

"Of course, baby." He couldn't help it, pressed his lips to her temple, and ducked to slide her carefully into the backseat. She curled up immediately on her side, struggling to breathe, and he touched her ankle before closing the door. He closed the other doors and left the car running though he cranked up the heat. "I'll be right back."

She didn't move or speak, though the hitch in her breathing betrayed she cried. He gritted his teeth against the keening cry that wanted to tell the world his mate suffered, and faced Edgar. "I'm taking her to her apartment. I'll stay until she feels better."

"We'll deal with this." Edgar canted his head at the unconscious manager at Atticus's feet. "Call if you need me to send the doc over to her place. There are some painkillers in the go bag, but they're probably way too strong. Might need x-rays or an ultrasound or something."

"Have the doc on standby. I'll call this afternoon." He strode back to the car and got in, listening closely for Natalia's breathing. Less panicked, but still uneven and labored. Logan said quietly, "We'll be home soon, I promise."

It took forever to get to her place, though in reality it was only fifteen or twenty minutes. She lived in one of the up-and-coming neighborhoods, in an apartment building in the shittier side of up-and-coming. It worked in his favor, though, because no one looked their way or asked any questions as he carried Natalia and the enormous duffel bag of supplies up the stairs to her third-floor studio. He stood her up and she leaned into him as he unlocked the door, then helped her limp inside. She headed straight for the bathroom without a word, and Logan locked the door behind him as he studied the apartment. The first thing he would do would be get better locks, deadbolts, and chains on the door. Well, the first and only thing he wanted was Natalia living in his house, where he knew she would be safe. If that didn't happen immediately, a solid door and strong locks — preferably in a new building with a concierge, security guard, and private garage — were a place to start.

No real decoration or personality marked the apartment as Natalia's, despite her scent lingering in every room. The furniture was battered but comfortable and clean, the television small and dusty. Every kitchen gadget imaginable cluttered the counters around the stove. Logan glanced into her fridge, then filled the kettle with water and placed it on the stove. Before he could turn on the burner, though, a thump from the bathroom distracted him. He went immediately to the door, hands braced on the frame as he leaned his forehead against the smooth wood. "Natalia? Are you okay?"

Only running water from the shower answered him.

Logan cleared his throat, shifting his feet and fighting the urge to break down the door. "Baby, are you okay? Do you need something?"

When her uneven breathing reached him through the sound of the water, he tried the doorknob. It opened, the door swinging in. She stood in the shower, fully clothed and shivering, and looked at him. Logan moved slowly to fuss with the water. "That water's freezing, Natalia."

It warmed against his arm as he steadied her, the chef still wobbly on her bruised legs. He didn't want to strip her down, but the sight of the ruined and bloody clothes made his lion roar and stalk. Logan took a deep breath and attempted a smile for her. "I'll get you some pajamas, okay? Take those dirty clothes off and I'll throw them out, and then you can finish washing your hair. Do you want some tea?"

She just looked at him, unblinking. Logan swallowed his impatience, his need to fix her right away, and concentrated on Edgar's words: what happened between them now would stay between them for the rest of their lives. He had to be careful. He had to be gentle. Those were not easy things for a lion.

chapter 7

My knees screamed as I ran to the bathroom, making it to the toilet just before I threw up coffee and scrambled eggs. I managed to brush my teeth, not looking in the mirror, and turned on the shower. My brain and body worked at odds — my thoughts slow and sluggish but every movement of my limbs too quick, too jerky. Uneven.

Everything felt wrong. I stepped into the shower and stood under the water, biting back a cry as the freezing stream hit the back of my head. I had to get the feel of him off me. Had to scrub away his fingerprints. I bumped the precariously-balanced shampoo bottle on the shelf, and it bounced off my foot and the tub. I put my hands over my face, and froze as a voice, warm and smooth as honey, cut through the door and the running water.

"Natalia? Are you okay?"

My heart jumped to my throat. Logan. I'd almost forgotten he was there. In my apartment. My crappy, messy apartment. My toes curled in the freezing water and I couldn't answer, teeth chattering together as I stared at the door.

He'd seen me terrified and incoherent in the alley, after Joey — I pushed away the thought and swallowed the panic. I was fine. He didn't hurt me. Logan drove me home, and I was safe. Safe.

The door creaked open and Logan looked for me, forehead creased. He stopped short when he saw me standing in the shower, then he reached for the knobs. "That water's freezing, Natalia."

Every part of me shook, from adrenaline or the cold water didn't really matter. But he was there, he was real. Solid and warm and careful, so damn careful — moving slow, staying quiet. The breath hitched in my throat. Logan frowned as he looked at me, said something about pajamas and tea. I didn't need pajamas and tea. I needed to be clean. I needed to know that men existed in the world who weren't like Joey.

He turned to go and I said, "Wait."

Relief etched across his face as he looked at me. And waited for me to speak more.

The bathroom filled with steam as the water warmed, and I closed my eyes so I couldn't see him as I said, "Can you — will you help me?"

"Of course, baby," he breathed, shut the door behind him. Got closer. "Just tell me how."

Baby. It warmed me from the inside as the water thawed my skin. I felt him get closer but didn't open my eyes. I pulled at my coat, the shirt underneath. "I can't get these off."

A long pause, then he took a deep breath. "You want me to help take your clothes off."

"You don't have to," I said. I struggled with the sodden coat, the weight pulling at my sore shoulder.

"Wait, wait." A rustle and soft thud had me open my eyes — he shed his coat and sweater and shoes but kept on the jeans and t-shirt underneath. Then he leaned into the spray of the shower and eased the coat off, tossing it to the floor in a soaking heap. He worked slowly, carefully, and narrated everything he intended before he touched me.

The warmth of the shower and the soothing quality of his voice lulled and relaxed me, and I wobbled. Reached out to catch myself on the tile and nearly pitched to my face. Logan made a noise and suddenly he was in the shower *with* me, clothes and all, and held me upright. I opened my eyes and looked up at him.

He smiled, leaning me against his chest and pretending he couldn't see every square inch of me. "What else can I help you with?"

I couldn't help it. I smiled back. I rested my cheek against the flat plane of his chest, the warm wet cotton of his t-shirt so soft against my skin I closed my eyes and rubbed against him. Almost drunk on him and the security of being in his arms. God help me. "I have to wash my hair. Get the b-blood out."

The thought of what stank up my hair brought the entire experience back, and I shuddered.

Logan rubbed my back and murmured, "I got you, don't even worry about it. Put your arms around me."

As if I needed an invitation, when I still nuzzled against his chest. My arms looped around his waist. I held my wrist and concentrated only on breathing along with the gentle rise and fall of his chest. He hummed, though it sounded more like a purr, and it rattled through me and chased away whatever badness remained from the morning.

He redirected the showerhead and rubbed my hair until it was soaking wet and probably snarled in a rat's nest. I just knew I'd spend the next week trying to comb it out again. But it didn't matter, not when he poured way too much shampoo on my head and the scent of coconut covered us both. His heart thumped a steady rhythm against my ear.

It was only the gentleness in him that let me speak. "You said you were sorry that you didn't get there sooner."

His hands paused, then returned to lathering my hair, massaging deep into my scalp and down my neck. His voice rumbled deep in his chest, not interrupting that purr for even a heartbeat. "I am sorry."

I tightened my death grip around his middle and sighed, moving my feet to a more comfortable stance. "I'm just grateful you came at all."

"I will always come when you call me," he said, fingers working my shoulders and down my spine until I felt boneless. "Natalia, if you need me, I will be there to protect you."

"Okay." I turned my head so I could press the other cheek against him.

"Okay," he repeated, then rinsed my hair. He didn't speak again until the water started to cool and no trace of soap remained, though Logan continued to massage the knots in my shoulders and back. "Can you sit by yourself for a second?"

I nodded, even though I wasn't entirely certain I could. The water stopped, the shower curtain moved, and then he wrapped me up in the enormous bath sheet that had been an indulgence from my first big paycheck. Logan gave wrapping up my wet hair a good try with a smaller towel, and finally settled for just covering it. He helped me step out of the tub and sit on the edge, rubbing my arms from shoulders to elbows. "I'll be right back."

He moved so damn quickly and silently for such a big guy. It seemed like I blinked and he was dripping wet in front of me, then another blink and he was gone, then another and he stood in front of me in dry clothes. Dry clothes? I looked up at him, confused, and he smiled with half his mouth. "Edgar is very well-prepared for every contingency."

Edgar. I nodded, about to speak, but he leaned down and picked me up, held me against his chest and the warm, clean-smelling white t-shirt. He carried me through the living area to my bed, still rumpled and unmade from this morning, and sat me upright on the end of it.

"Will you thank Edgar for me? And Atticus?" I cleared my throat to clear a sudden lump. "For helping when —"

"Of course," he said, palm warm and comforting against my arm. "Of course I will."

He propped all of my pillows up around me, frowning in concentration as he created a nest with the comforter and an extra blanket from the couch. I watched his face in fascination. Something about his features seemed different — his cheekbones more pronounced, maybe, or his mouth a little wider. His hair looked longer, more golden.

Logan retrieved a giant black duffel bag, no doubt Edgar's supplies, and crouched in front of me. He examined my bruised and bloodied knees, the egg-sized lumps on each, and probed them gently before glancing up at me. "How bad do they hurt?"

"Not so much any more," I breathed, mesmerized. His eyes were definitely not brown. They were brilliant gold, almost reflecting the sunlight from the east-facing window back at me.

He smiled and that rumble started in his chest again. "That's good."

Logan smeared cool antibiotic cream across the scrapes, careful not to get any on the sheets, then covered them with gauze and stretchy wrap bandages. The only sound was the hush-hush of his breathing and that crazy purr as he picked up my hands, examining my wrists and elbows for any other evidence of violence. My breath hitched and he looked at my face, worry in the lines around his eyes, but the purr grew louder and I smiled, a little puzzled.

His fingers slid under my chin and he tilted my face, peering at my cheek and jaw. Logan spread more of the cream across a scrape on my jaw, near my cheek, then plastered a bandaid across it. He still held my jaw.

Time slowed to a crawl, and I leaned forward, searching his eyes for a hint of why he helped me. Why he cared enough to give me a bandaid for a tiny scratch. He stopped breathing as my lips brushed his, as my palms rested on his cheeks, drew him closer. I closed my eyes, pressed my mouth against his soft lips again. His hand slid to the back of my neck, drew me closer. I melted against him.

An eternity passed in a blink, and he retreated, stroked my cheek and my throat and across my bare collarbone. Logan took a deep breath and kissed my forehead, my jaw, behind my ear. Made a strangled noise in his throat before holding my face carefully. His eyes were definitely gold, radiating their own sunlight at me. "There's time for more of that later."

"Now is a good time," I said. Drunk on him, on everything about him.

He smiled, ducked his head to hide it but couldn't as he looked back at me. "Not when you're wearing just a towel, baby. And you need to rest. You should take some ibuprofen for sure, and I have painkillers if you want them."

He was right. Everything felt strange and off, as if I moved under deep water. Kissing him on my bed was not a good idea, even worse when I was naked. My voice still came out hoarse. "Just the ibuprofen."

Logan retrieved a glass of water and a bottle of pills, shaking a few into my palm and watching as I swallowed them. He nudged me to lay back but I frowned, rubbing my sore shoulder. "Clothes. I need something to wear."

He glanced at his phone as it rang, then pulled another t-shirt, sweatshirt, and enormous sweatpants from the duffel bag. "These?"

I laughed, holding the towel with one hand as I held up the t-shirt. "Seriously?"

"I like the thought of you wearing my clothes," he said, then ducked to kiss my forehead. "Only if you want to. I have to take this; it's Edgar. I'll be right outside, just shout if you need anything."

He strode for the door, a completely different man as he barked into the phone, "What?" and closed the door solidly behind himself.

I looked at where he'd gone, swallowing hard. Then I staggered to my feet, holding the towel against my chest as I hobbled to the dresser to retrieve panties and sports bra and yoga pants. But I pulled on his shirt, because I liked the idea of wearing his clothes, too.

chapter 8

Logan stood in the hall outside Natalia's apartment, scowling enough he thought all the bones in his face would break. "Say that again."

Edgar's laconic voice only made him want to put his fist through the wall. "The manager was laundering money through the restaurant. Something about the deliveries being used to cycle cash through the kitchen. He's in deep with a loan shark or two, from what I can gather. The former owner claims he knows nothing about it, but I don't believe him. I can push harder if you want."

When Edgar said push harder, that usually meant people ended up in the hospital. Logan pinched the bridge of his nose, wanting only to be curled up around Natalia in her bed. "Not yet. Which loan sharks does he owe?"

"Bridger and Hanover so far. He won't admit to anyone else."

"We have a meeting?"

"Yep." Edgar spoke to someone in the background, then returned his attention to the phone. "At the restaurant in half an hour. If you want to handle this yourself, great. If not, I will make our interest in the restaurant and the chef's personal safety abundantly clear."

"I'll be there." Logan glanced at Natalia's door, wishing he had time to put new locks on it. "Make sure the manager is there as well. I want to make sure he understands the message. Have Carter pick up new door hardware. Deadbolts and a chain at least."

"Locking someone in somewhere?" The laugh in Edgar's voice would have gotten anyone else punched through the phone.

As it was, Logan only gritted his teeth. "She lives in a shitty part of town. Until I can convince her to move somewhere safer, the door gets reinforced. I'll buy the damn building if I have to. Have Carter wait until I'm back at her place, then he can start work."

"Good enough. See you in a few." The line went dead.

Logan listened at the door for a moment being entering the apartment. Natalia lay curled up in her bed, the careful nest he'd constructed around her disassembled. She was completely covered from head to toe, from socks all the way to the towel still wrapping her damp hair. He refilled the glass of water and left the bottle of pills on the small table next to the bed, crouching to rest his chin on the mattress. She opened her eyes and smiled drowsily. "You're back."

"I'm back." He stroked her cheek, trying to memorize every detail of her face. "But I have to go take care of some business, okay? I'll be back in an hour. You rest. And use this if you need anything." He took the burner phone from the duffel bag and left it on the mattress right next to her hand. "My number is programmed, so are Edgar's and Atticus's. If you need anything — *anything*, Natalia — call. Any of us."

"Sure," she sighed, eyes drifting shut again. He knew perfectly well it was the adrenaline crash and the cold and just a bad morning that made her so tired, but it still sparked concern in his chest.

He would have given his entire fortune just to crawl in next to her and keep her warm. But the only way to guarantee her safety and the safety of that restaurant was to make it clear to the loan sharks that Logan Chase would not tolerate anything untoward. So he forced himself to walk out and lock the door behind him.

Every mile he drove away from her made his skin crawl. By the time he reached the restaurant, he verged on a shift. It took several minutes in the car, concentrating on breathing exercises, to make sure he didn't go full lion in the back alley. Benedict waited patiently on the loading dock, carrying the folio of legal documents he wielded as effectively as Atticus used his fists. Logan forced himself to get out of the car, ignoring Benedict's raised eyebrows at his attire. Normally Logan wouldn't be caught dead outside a gym in sweatpants, but his jeans still occupied a corner of Natalia's bathroom floor. And he didn't mind for a second that his clothes marked her apartment as part of his territory.

"Well?"

Benedict glanced at his papers. "The only complication that might arise is whether any of the illicit funds benefited the soup kitchen. It looks like our friend Joseph was a fairly incompetent money launderer, but I don't think either Bridger or Hanover knew how bad he was at it."

"Are they here yet?"

"Not yet."

"Good. Let's go." He stormed across the loading dock and into the back of the restaurant, through the kitchen to the dining room. Atticus stood over the manager, who looked much the worse for wear, while Edgar taped a sign to the door that said the restaurant was closed for two days.

Benedict nodded to his brothers and spoke quietly to Edgar before returning to the manager's office, no doubt to start calling employees. Logan paused long enough to tell him to assure the employees they would still receive their full pay for the two days the restaurant was not operating, then turned his attention to the dirtbag manager.

Cold fury turned his insides to ice, and it took every ounce of control in him to keep from just killing the man. The manager's lank hair fell across his forehead, almost obscuring the bruises and cuts from Atticus's attention, and his hands were bound to the legs of the chair. He still looked pretty self-assured, despite the rough treatment.

The manager grunted. "So you're the bankroll? Look, dude, whoever you are —"

"Don't speak." Edgar said it absently, as if he'd repeated it several times already, and didn't look up from where he reviewed the night's reservations.

Logan cracked his knuckles. "They coming to the front or the back?"

"Front." Edgar glanced up, then canted his head for Logan to join him at the maître d' station. He tapped the stack of schematics he examined, and it took Logan only a moment to recognize a security plan. "They'll be here any second. I don't anticipate either giving us trouble. But in anticipation for this idiot's other debts coming around to us, I drew up a new plan for cameras, alarms, and a few other tricks."

"Good." Logan stared unseeing at the drawings, the lists of equipment. "Buy it, install it as soon as possible. Tomorrow is too late. And every night that she's here, one of our guys is as well. In the kitchen or the back or at a damn table — someone we trust is here."

"Not a problem." When Logan gave him a look, Edgar raised an eyebrow. "One soufflé and there will be a list of volunteers from across the company. I don't think you'll have to worry about it." He got up and went to unlock the front door. "Looks like our company is here."

The manager laughed. "You guys are in for it, you don't know who —"

He silenced with a grunt, and when Logan looked back, Atticus stood there serenely.

Bridger and Hanover ran all sorts of illicit businesses though their bread and butter was loaning enormous amounts of money to people they knew probably couldn't pay it back. Then they blackmailed the victims into joining or facilitating their schemes. Like the shithead manager laundering money through a legitimate restaurant.

The man, Hanover, looked like an accountant — slight, bookish, wearing half-moon glasses on the end of his nose as he ducked into the dim restaurant and blinked. The disarming appearance was all a facade, though — the man was ruthless. Absolutely ruthless. He ordered assassinations and disappearances as easily as he might have ordered one of Natalia's soufflés. His partner, Bridger, looked like any small town beauty queen and even talked with a drawl. She was even worse than Hanover.

Edgar locked the door behind them, and the manager started to pull at his bound hands. "Hanover, man, you gotta —"

Again, Atticus silenced him.

Hanover frowned thoughtfully as he looked around the restaurant. "Joseph? Whatever is this —" He cut off when he saw Atticus, then took a step back as his gaze drifted to Logan and Edgar. Hanover licked his lips, hand a little shaky as he brushed at his comb-over. "Oh my. Mr. Chase. Whatever is the matter?"

"Sit." Edgar pulled out a chair at one of the tables, close enough that the manager could hear and remember, though the man's jaw hung slack at the loan shark's reaction to Logan and his brothers.

Hanover sat immediately, as did Bridger — although she smiled as she walked past Atticus, her fingers trailing across his chest until Atticus's face flushed. Logan seated himself across from them, resting his hands on the smooth white tablecloth before he spoke. "We have a slight conflict of interest to resolve, Mr. Hanover."

Always better to start polite. Hanover and Bridger dabbled in loans to some of the shifters and were engaged in some other questionable betting, including on the illegal fights that some shifters ran. They knew enough to cause him some trouble, although the trouble would only last until Atticus got his hands on them.

"I can assure you, Mr. Chase," Bridger started, her voice a husky purr intended to lure hapless men into stupid business decisions. She even gave him a look at her cleavage, playing with her necklace. "Our interests will never conflict with yours. If there was perhaps a — misunderstanding? — we can correct that. Easily."

"Good." Logan sat back as the familiar corporate raider mask settled over him. "I purchased this restaurant two days ago. The chef is a friend of mine."

"Natalia Spencer," Hanover said, thin lips twitching. "She's very talented. Congratulations."

A bead of sweat broke out on the man's forehead, and Bridger looked a little uncertain.

Logan nodded, fingers drumming on the table. "Indeed. Unfortunately, there have been some ... irregularities in the day to day management of the restaurant that have caused my accountants and lawyers some consternation."

Bridger looked over her shoulder at Joey, her expression hard. "I'm sure we can explain any irregularities, Mr. Chase."

The manager stared between them all as if he couldn't quite understand what was being said. Logan didn't allow himself to celebrate. "I'm glad. While I understand this restaurant was used in the past to accommodate some of your more sensitive requirements, I can't have that occur any longer. I hope that is not too inconvenient for you."

"Not at all." Hanover cleared his throat, sitting forward until his dark eyes glinted in the dim room. "May I ask, Mr. Chase, how, uh, thorough are your accountants?"

"Very."

The thin man's face paled still more, and another bead of sweat joined the first on his forehead. "I see. I do see."

"But they are also quite discreet." Logan held out his hand, and Edgar, standing behind him, placed a file in his hand. It may or may not have contained anything useful, but they didn't know that. "As of this morning, I am the only person in possession of the previous financial records for this establishment. That's how it will stay, so long as our interests no longer intersect at this restaurant. I hope that is agreeable?"

"Quite." Bridger toyed with one of her long earrings, her eyes dead and flat as a shark's as she studied him. "We appreciate your discretion."

"I thought you would." Logan frowned at the manager sitting off to the side, and his fingers continued their muffled tattoo against the table. "As a professional courtesy, though, I would offer a bit of insight into what my accountants found. The manager is sloppy. Lazy and wasteful. His fingerprints, yours, and those of your vendors are all over every transaction that occurred. Had someone audited this company, I've no doubt you would both have a lot of uncomfortable questions to answer."

Annoyance tinged Bridger's expression. "Is that a fact. Thank you for bringing it to our attention."

They looked ready to go, itching to get at their books and the manager to figure out what type of cleanup they had to do, but Logan moved his hand and they froze. He chose his words with care. "On a personal note. Ms. Spencer is very special to me." He glared at them until both the loan sharks nodded, clear in his meaning, and only then did Logan go on, pointing at the manager. "This morning, when she discovered something amiss with the delivery and called me, your employee attacked her. Tried to rape her or kill her."

He paused to let the rage settle before it choked him and was only somewhat surprised at the disgust in Bridger's face. Logan went on, keeping his voice quiet so they wouldn't know he was at the end of his control. "Luckily for him and you, my brothers were close enough to handle the situation. Had I arrived first, you would be cleaning up pieces of your employee from the loading dock. The piece of shit continues to threaten her and inferred he would return to the restaurant at some point to even the score."

"I assure you, Mr. Chase, that will certainly never happen." Hanover removed a plain white handkerchief from inside his suit jacket, patting at his forehead. "We will have a talk with Joseph."

"See that you do." Logan glanced inside the prop folder, then closed it and handed it back to Edgar. "If I see him near this restaurant, or within half a mile of Ms. Spencer, the repercussions will reflect not only on him but on you. None of us want that."

"No," Bridger said.

"I hope we understand each other." Logan rose, done with the meeting and ready to be back with Natalia, hopefully before she woke up alone. He shook their hands briefly, letting them feel that he could crush every bone in their bodies without much effort.

"We do, Mr. Chase, we certainly do." Hanover scowled as he looked at the sullen manager. "I am terribly sorry for the inconvenience. We will certainly make the gravity of the situation clear to Joseph. Please pass our sincerest apologies to Ms. Spencer. If there are any expenses associated with her treatment, please do pass them along, and we will be pleased to cover them."

"Not necessary, but thank you." Logan watched Atticus untie the manager and propel him out the front door with a little more force than necessary, though neither Bridger nor Hanover seemed concerned when the manager flew face-first into a light post. The loan sharks strode out and turned in separate directions. A dark sedan rolled up and an enormous man, probably their Atticus, picked Joseph up and threw him in the trunk before speeding off.

Edgar locked the door, closed the shades, and looked at Logan. "I gather you're busy for the rest of the day?"

"At least. Have Carter head toward her apartment, and once Benedict is done with the books here, I want to find a better apartment for her. Closer. I'll talk to her about moving later, but I'd rather have the options ready to go."

"Got it." Edgar frowned at the paperwork in his hands though he didn't seem to see any of it. His voice lowered. "How is she?"

Logan rubbed his face, sighing. "In pain, bruised. Scared. Tired. She was resting when I left. I'll give you a call later. You can bring dinner over if you want."

"Just let me know." Edgar gathered his things and went to find Benedict, and Logan made a beeline to the door.

Atticus followed on his heels, hands shoved in his pockets. "I'll come with Edgar, if that's okay? I want to make sure she's okay."

Logan nodded, slapping his shoulder. "Of course, At."

Then he was at the car, driving as fast as he could back to where Natalia, his mate, slept.

chapter 9

I woke as the door opened, and my hand tightened around the phone Logan left. I lifted my head, then exhaled as I saw him creep through the door and lock it behind him. He smiled sheepishly. "Sorry to wake you. How do you feel?"

"Terrible." I buried my face in the pillow. "Everything hurts."

He took his shoes off near the door and approached, digging something else out of the duffel bag before sitting on the mattress next to my hips. He rattled another bottle of pills. "Half of one?"

I tried to sit and the breath hissed in my teeth as my shoulder and back objected. I took the half white pill he handed me, gulping it down before I tried to wiggle out of bed. "I should go —" and I trailed off, looking at the bathroom door but not wanting to announce that all the coffee I'd had before the incident was coming back to haunt me.

Logan immediately picked me up and carried me the twenty feet to the bathroom, and I laughed. "I can walk, thank you."

"Not if I'm here," he said, putting me on my feet and opening the door for me. "I don't want you to fall or trip or bump yourself."

I shook my head and hobbled through the disaster of wet clothes and towels in the bathroom to take care of business. He stood at the front door, talking to someone, when I limped back out. Carter leaned around his brother and looked at me a little mournfully. "Hi Natalia. Are you okay?"

My chest constricted. The feeling of Joey's arm against my throat, choking me, rushed back, and I froze. I struggled to smile, hugging myself. "Yeah. Thanks for asking, Carter."

Logan almost closed the door in his face as he returned to help me back to bed.

I tried to smile as I eased into bed, though I lay on my side facing away from him. "Have to get over it eventually."

He touched my shoulder, the lightest touch before retreating. "At your own speed. He's changing the locks on your door, adding a chain and a few other things. So you'll be safer."

Tears prickled my eyes. I might not have told him, but the flimsy door bothered me even before Joey attacked me. I cleared my throat. "Thank you."

"What else can I do to make you safe?" He touched my tangled hair, my back, almost desperate to comfort me. "Natalia, tell me. Please."

The painkiller, whatever it was, slowed everything down again and lowered a fog around me. Everything felt warm and close. Sleep beckoned as the sharp agony in my knees and shoulder faded to a dull throb. I managed to reach a hand back to him. "Will you lie down with me?"

"Of course." His weight dipped the mattress behind me, the sheets and blankets rustling and moving as he settled. Logan spooned me, pulled me close to his chest and draped his arm over my side until he covered me almost as closely as the sheets did. He arranged the pillows and blanket, absently kissing the back of my neck. "Are you comfortable?"

"Cold," I murmured. My eyes wouldn't stay open, lead weights dragging my lids down. I wiggled and relaxed, sighing.

"That I can help with," he said. Drew me closer and that delicious rumble sparked in his chest, tickling me as he breathed deeply from my hair.

"You purr a lot," I said. I pressed my face against the pillow of his arm. He felt like a furnace, warming me all the way through until cold was a distant memory.

The rumble quieted. He said something that I didn't catch, a narcotic haze dragging me away. I yawned and stretched, then settled closer to him. "You smell good."

"So do you," he murmured, voice husky. His mouth left a trail of kisses along my neck and behind my ear. "Distractingly good. Go to sleep, baby. We can talk when you're feeling better."

It sounded like a good idea. Darkness settled around me, despite the tinkering sounds from the door, and I yawned again. "I feel better with you here."

"I'm glad." His arm tightened around my middle, held me securely in the curve of his body. "I feel better that I'm here, too."

I meant to say more, to thank him for everything, but I opened my mouth and everything went dark.

Logan dozed as he held Natalia, only moving when he needed to wake her. She had nightmares at least twice that he noticed, once crying out in fear before he managed to soothe her back to an easy sleep. Carter finished quickly with the door and crept close enough to ask if Logan needed anything else, then left.

It felt right, the quiet thump-thump of her heartbeat reassuring against his arm and the scent of her hair and skin curling around him. His lion purred, settled down finally to know she was as protected as he could make her. So far. Logan ran his fingers along her forearm, learning the curves and bumps of her wrist, as he planned. A new apartment and a new car, since the clunker she drove looked like a deathtrap just waiting to fall apart. With winter coming, something more solid, with better tires and handling, would be necessary. A two-bedroom apartment, he amended, closer to the restaurant. Walking distance to the restaurant, maybe. Secure lobby, concierge and security, access-controlled garage.

He glanced around the apartment, frowning. New furniture, definitely. And a gourmet kitchen, of course. Logan shushed her as Natalia stirred, uneasy, and she tried to sit, "Logan?"

"I'm here," he said, tightening his arms around her. "I've got you."

"Oh." Natalia relaxed and drifted off again without another word, and Logan smiled.

He was lost. He knew it. His voice came out a little rusty as he went on, murmuring his plans to her and hoping the sound of his voice would reassure her even in her dreams. "I have big plans for us, sweetheart."

Her forehead wrinkled as she frowned, then burrowed further under the covers.

Logan closed his eyes as well. "First, we'll finish with the restaurant — better security to start, and then new appliances in the kitchen. Improve the gas lines and plumbing and everything so it's a better place for you to work. A new manager, of course. More staff. A throne for you to occupy and direct your minions." He chuckled at the thought though it seemed entirely in character that she would perch on a high chair and shake a spatula — or carving knife — to order her cooks around.

He continued his mental list, glad he could talk through the process aloud, even though she was unconscious. "And then we'll get you settled somewhere much nicer, much safer. A penthouse suite, maybe. Two bedrooms, so you can have visitors. A beautiful kitchen and a beautiful view for my beautiful chef." He kissed her neck and shoulder, loving the taste of her skin. "Until you're ready to move in with me." It came out softer, a little less certain.

It felt too vulnerable, asking her to live with him, to be his, without knowing the answer for certain. It had only been a few days, less than a week, from the moment they met — and she hadn't liked him for most of that time. Only in the last day or two did she seem to tolerate him. He knew most humans wouldn't be as certain about the rightness of being together after only a few days, and wondered how long he would have to wait until she really understood who and what he was.

"Maybe," he said to her hair, tangling his fingers with hers. "Maybe I could move in with you in that big new apartment. We could live there together. Stay at the mansion on the weekends, maybe, if you're not working."

"Walk-in closet," she said, sighed against his arm.

Logan went still, wondering how much she heard. He brushed the hair away from her face, trying to see her expression. "What, baby?"

"I always wanted a walk-in closet," she said.

"I'll get you two." Logan kissed her cheek, touched her chin so he could see her face. "Would you live with me, Natalia? At my house or a new apartment or somewhere we both choose? Stay with me and be mine?"

She stretched, wiggling onto her back and looking up at him with sleepy eyes. "What about your brothers?"

"What about them?" He smiled, kissed the corner of her mouth.

"Where would they live?"

"Wherever they want," Logan said. He remained on his side, not wanting to loom over her. "Are you feeling better?"

"Still sore." Her eyes drooped, her cheeks flushed with warmth and the sunlight streaming in the windows. "Tired."

"We're not going anywhere today," he said. Logan couldn't stop touching her, studying the delicate bones of her clavicle and brushing the tips of his fingers across her throat. "So other than a walk-in closet, what should we look for?"

She stretched again, and the t-shirt she wore — his t-shirt — ruffled up and exposed smooth, soft skin. The yoga pants did nothing to hide the gentle swell of her hip and stomach, evidence of a life of indulgence and enjoyment. Thank God, finally a woman who loved food. Loved wine and eating decadent food late into the night and sleeping in.

Natalia fussed with the sheets for a moment before settling back down. "Gas range. That's it."

A laugh bounced through him and escaped, and Logan bumped his forehead to hers as Natalia smiled in response. He examined a scrape on her elbow that he hadn't seen before, trying not to laugh too much. "That's it? A walk-in closet and a gas range and you're happy?"

"Mmm." She relaxed again and seemed to sleep, a very soft snore rattling in her throat.

Logan sighed as he studied her face, tracing the line of her nose and mouth and eyebrows over and over. The next time he looked up at the clock, it was late afternoon and his stomach growled. Natalia still slept, tangled up in the sheets, but instead of laying curled up in a self-protected ball, she sprawled across the entire mattress. She winced occasionally when her knees bumped something, but otherwise she rested well.

He extricated himself from the comfort of the bed and padded over to the kitchen. He texted Edgar to bring food soon, and then gathered up all the wet clothes and towels from the bathroom. It took him a moment to look around and realize she didn't have a washer or dryer. Those made his list for the new apartment. No more schlepping things to a laundromat or dicey laundry room in the basement of a building. Irritated, he hung everything up to drip-dry over the tub.

When he returned to the main room, he found Natalia sitting up in bed, looking confused. Her expression cleared when she saw him. "Oh."

Logan raised an eyebrow as he went to the kitchen and lit the burner under the teakettle. "What's the matter, babe?"

The flush rose in her cheeks. "I thought maybe I dreamed you."

"Well, I *am* dreamy," he said, deadpan.

Natalia made a pained noise as she slid to the edge of the mattress and tried to stand, but when Logan moved to help her, she held up a hand. "I can do it."

So he stood back as she hobbled to the bathroom, cursing with each step. As much as he enjoyed caring for her, he knew she wouldn't appreciate it all the time. He stood in the kitchen, staring at the door that separated her from him, and willed himself to calm. It helped that Edgar arrived before Natalia reappeared, his brother carrying bags of takeout containers to set on the counter in the kitchen.

Logan started unpacking the white cartons of rice and Thai food. "Where's Atticus?"

"Kept him at the restaurant, supervising the install. One of the manager's vendors showed up, interested in reinvigorating his relationship with the new ownership. I thought it best to keep the kid there in case skulls needed cracking."

Logan gritted his teeth. "I thought we made things clear this morning."

"We did. To Bridger and Hanover." Edgar frowned as he searched for plates and bowls, rubbing his jaw as he set them out. "But the manager wasn't just doing deals with them. He had side deals with some shady characters, buying meat and produce that mostly fell off other people's trucks. He pocketed the cash the owner set aside to pay for actual ingredients and replaced it with utter trash. It's amazing your chef was as successful as she was."

"Yeah." Logan glanced at the closed door but kept his voice low just in case she would overhear before he had a chance to review their earlier conversation. "Any luck finding an apartment?"

"I put Carter on it. There are a couple of options near the restaurant, but it's an in-demand location. You'll pay for it."

"It needs a walk-in closet. Two walk-in closets." He felt like an idiot under Edgar's amused scrutiny but refused to show it. "And a gas range. Two bedrooms. A fireplace. Big shower, big bathtub. Those are the requirements."

"Hers or yours?" Edgar snorted, his normally impassive expression cracking with a smile. "Give me the budget, and I'll have Jen from the real estate office take Natalia around. Otherwise, it'll take months to find something."

Logan froze as Natalia said, "Who's taking me where?"

She'd exited the bathroom quietly enough neither of them heard — although, from the look on Edgar's face, Logan suspected maybe his brother *had* heard. Logan gave him a look before pulling out a chair from the cafe table near the kitchen. "Sit, babe. I thought it would be nice if we found a new apartment. Some place closer to the restaurant, so you could walk to work if you wanted."

Her head tilted, eyes narrowed. "We?"

His heart sank. "You don't remember talking about that?"

She sighed, rubbing the back of her neck, and sank into the chair. "I thought you were kidding."

Edgar placed a bowl of rice on the table in front of her, saying, "He never kids," before retrieving the containers of curry, pad thai, drunken noodles, and other mysterious chicken concoctions.

"I see that," Natalia said, tone dry. She pointed her spoon at Logan. "Since you drugged me up the last time we talked about this, let's review. Why should I live with you?"

"Because I love you." It slipped out before Logan could think of a better response, so he let the words hang there in the air between them. Her eyebrows climbed toward her hairline, and even Edgar took a step back. Logan waited.

She laughed, flustered. "You can't be serious."

"He's always serious," Edgar said, then clapped Logan on the shoulder. "And I should be going. Natalia, I'm glad to see you up and about. Let me know if there's anything I can do for you." He disappeared out the door, and Logan watched Natalia, bracing for the sharp words.

Instead, she just stared at him, spoon forgotten in her hand. He watched her think, holding his breath, and wondered how long he would have to wait to hear her say the words back to him.

After an eternity of silence, she turned her attention to the panang curry in front of her. "Did anyone print the menus for this week?"

Irritated, Logan sat down across from her. "No."

"Good." She licked her spoon, attention on the bowl in front of her. "I don't like it when people make decisions for me. I'm not a control freak but for the restaurant, for my life — I want to decide." She fixed him with an even look, words weighty but placed with care. "I hope you understand that. I make my own decisions. I won't be bullied into anything."

"Good." Logan gripped the edge of the table to keep from breaking something in his fists. "Since I'm not a bully."

She made a noncommittal noise, and Logan sighed. "Fine. I won't bully *you*."

A hint of a smile, there and gone like a hummingbird. “Okay.”

“Okay what?”

“Okay, I’ll live with you.”

The lion started rumbling, wanting to hold her again, to pin her underneath him. Logan sat back in his chair, eyebrow raised. “And why are you going to live with me?”

Mischief made her eyes darker as she studied her spoon, nonchalant. “I might, you know, love you too. Maybe.”

“I can live with maybe. For a little while.” Logan got up to pour them tea, though he wished for a bottle of whiskey instead. He still clinked his cup to hers once he was back at the table, trying not to grin like a fool. “To a new adventure in a nicer part of town.”

She smiled, and he didn’t mind looking like a fool at all.

chapter 10

Three days later I wanted to call it off, to stay in my crappy tiny apartment and not look at another shiny building in my life. Jen, the realtor, was distressingly bubbly and a morning person to boot. She spoke more words before eight a.m. than I did all day. After our first encounter, she didn't call before nine and always, always brought me coffee. She was very concerned that Mr. Chase knew she did everything in her power to make me happy, and after the constant references to Mr. Chase and his brothers, Mr. Chase and his excellent taste, Mr. Chase and his request for multiple closets, I was ready to punt Mr. Chase to the curb and find my own place.

But she meant well and seemed a genuinely nice person, so it was difficult to be too mean to her. My frustration grew out of the multitude of options and Logan's seeming indifference to the acceptable ones. He wanted the perfect one. He wanted an apartment that had everything, that was the best in the city — whether it was for sale or not. He only wanted the penthouse. Anything else wasn't good enough. Since there were limited buildings near the restaurant, that meant Jen had her work cut out for her trying to make the current owners sell or move.

When I complained, as Logan and I ate lunch in the restaurant's kitchen, he shrugged and said the other solution was to look farther from the restaurant, but that would mean I needed a new car. Just the thought of trying to purchase a new car had me holding my hands up in surrender. It felt like everything happened too fast, an intense rush of emotions and change. Like I turned around and no longer recognized my life.

The changes at the restaurant were for the better, at least. Carter took over as manager, and with Logan Chase's connections, the quality and behavior of our vendors improved immediately. We hired more staff for the kitchen and started renovating the back of the house to replace all the shitty appliances Joey sold out from under us.

Even standing near the heat of the cooktops in the soup kitchen, thinking about him made me shiver. Logan and Edgar both promised he was dealt with, but I didn't entirely believe them. Joey was too mean to just disappear. Maybe the people he owed money figured that out, but I remembered from much earlier in my life that dead men didn't pay back debts. His loan sharks had no reason to kill him since that would eliminate his ability to pay. He was out there somewhere.

"More chicken noodle?" I added more herbs to the giant stockpot, then nodded to one of the volunteers. "This one's ready, take it out to the line."

The weather turned and grew blustery rather that just cool, and snow threatened. All of the shelters filled quickly, and the soup kitchen's clientele expanded just as fast. Logan thought I hadn't noticed, but the soup kitchen received a sizable donation that filled and re-filled the pantry. When I asked where the money came from, the charity that ran the facility only said it came from heaven. I snorted, concentrating on the next vat of broth and noodles. Heaven my ass, it had Logan's fingerprints all over it.

When I took a day or two off from the restaurant, Logan suggested — gently but insistently — that Jake take over as head chef for that time. I agreed, more so that Jake got the experience, but part of me was so exhausted from all the work of the last few years that I might have agreed with any reason Logan handed me. But it left me with more time to volunteer at the soup kitchen, despite that Logan complained he intended the time off from work to mean more time with him.

I hid a smile as he chopped fruit on the cutting board behind me, looking dead sexy in a hairnet and latex gloves. My suggestion that he spend time with me at the soup kitchen had not met with a great deal of enthusiasm, but I had to give him credit — he showed up. After his first attempt at fixing chili, though, I put him to doing something he couldn't burn or scald. He muttered and pouted about it, clearly having never been told he wasn't successful, but he did it. Obeying did not come naturally to him.

"How's it going?" I peered around his side, resting my head against his shoulder in a brief moment of weakness since all the volunteers were out serving the food. His grumbly noise started up the moment I touched him, and I breathed him in. I loved that sound.

He tried to sound dignified. "Very well, thank you. I'm a master with a knife, as these apples clearly demonstrate." He gestured at a pile of uneven apple chunks.

I bit my lip to keep from laughing at him and rubbed his back. "Thank you for trying."

"Shit." He laughed, giving me a sideways look. "That means I'm terrible at this too, doesn't it?"

"I don't think anyone out there will judge your apple cutting skills."

"You will, though." Logan raised his eyebrows.

"Never." When he just looked at me, I laughed and turned back to the soup. "Maybe a little. We'll have a knives class soon. Help with your technique."

Logan followed me, and his arms slid around my waist so he could draw me back against him, and that contented rumble vibrated through me. He kissed the side of my neck, the rough stubble of his jaw dragged shivers through me from head to toe. "I don't usually need help with technique, baby."

I snorted, trying to bump him back with my hip and elbow so I didn't catch fire on the burner, and peered at the batch of chicken noodle in front of me. "Such confidence, friend."

He made a hungry noise and nibbled behind my ear. His palm slid over my stomach, down to the waist of my jeans, and my breath caught. His voice grew rough. "After we're done here, how about drinks and a late dinner at my house? I'll cook."

"You have terrible taste," I said, breathless but trying not to show him how my stomach wobbled and dropped to my feet. "Why would I trust you in a kitchen?"

"By cook," he murmured, moving to kiss my other shoulder. "I meant cut fruit. You'll have fruit salad for dinner and like it."

I laughed but pulled away, giving him a look as I set the ladle aside. "Nice try."

"Babe, help me understand."

I paused, then shook my head. "What do you mean?"

"Natalia." When I glanced over, he leaned against the counter near his cutting board, arms folded over his chest. That patient look on his face that made my palms sweat. "You pull away when I touch you."

"It's not you." I tried to smile and concentrated on dicing more chicken in quick, efficient chops. "It's not *about* you, I mean."

"Tell me what's wrong. Tell me how to fix it."

I threw the chicken into the pot and stripped off my gloves, tossing them into the overflowing trashcan before I hauled it out and tied it off. "You can't fix it, Logan. You've already fixed everything else, pretty much, but this isn't

—" I took a deep breath and forced myself to meet his gaze steadily. "I just need time. It's not easy for me to trust someone like you."

His head cocked to the side. "Someone like me?"

"Rich. Handsome. Confident. Male. Terrible in a kitchen." I tried to smile as I dragged the trash to the back door. "I think dinner at your place would be nice, but I'll cook. But I don't want to sleep over."

Sleepover. Like we were children and had sleeping bags to roll out on the living room floor.

He straightened from his lean and reached for the trash. "Let me take that."

"I've got it." I kicked the door open, glad for the blast of cool air that chased the embarrassment from my cheeks. "Need some fresh air."

He caught my wrist before I could flee, though, and leaned to press his lips gently to mine. He caressed my cheek and then kissed the tip of my nose. "No pressure, babe. Just tell me if it's something I've done."

My heart surged in gratitude that he wasn't complaining about how we'd been going out for almost two weeks and I hadn't fucked him. I smiled, "Thank you," and shouldered the door back open. The alley was welcome space and open air and cool calm, and I heaved the trash into the dumpster despite the twinge from my shoulder.

I brushed my hands off and kneaded my lower back, looking up at the sky for a moment and wondering if there were shooting stars streaking across the sky.

"I told you this wasn't over."

Every muscle in my body seized up. For a moment, fear paralyzed me and I couldn't face the speaker — Joey, standing in the alley next to the dumpster. Holding a length of pipe in his hand and looking much the worse for wear. Yellow and purple bruises covered every visible inch of his face and throat, and a few of his fingers were splinted together. He smacked the pipe against his palm. "I'm going to break your legs first, so you can't run away."

I swallowed terror and backed toward the door. "Get the fuck away from me."

"Every moment of misery in the last two weeks is because of you. Everything was fine until you stuck your bitchy nose into my business and started calling around town. Well. Your fucking bodyguards aren't around tonight, are they?"

"Fuck. Off." I turned, wrenched at the door. Locked. I ducked, tried to dodge as the pipe thudded against the brick wall, and I kicked back.

He staggered, threw the pipe at my knees, and I screamed — more rage than pain, though. This son of a bitch was not going to hurt me. He was not going to win. He sure as shit wasn't going to violate the last place I actually felt safe. I picked the pipe up and whipped it at his head. "Get the fuck away from me. You're nothing. You're scum. I hope you fucking *die*, that your bookies rip your face off."

"Bitch," he snarled and lunged at me.

I meant to knee him in the groin and punch him in the nose, throw him into the dumpster and run around to the safety of the soup kitchen's brightly-lit windows. Instead, as Joey's stiff fingers clutched at my hair, the door to the kitchen blew open. Bent and folded as if it weren't solid metal.

I staggered back, about to scream again, but the sound died in my throat.

A cat, an enormous cat — a fucking *lion* stood over Joey, a massive paw planted on his chest. The lion roared, a sound that belonged in a nature documentary about Africa, not the back alley in an American city. I choked for breath, retreating to the other side of the alley as the thing snarled. Joey screamed and went silent, bloody rents in his chest staining the broken concrete of the ground. The lion, pretty much at eye-level with me as it turned, stalked closer. My knees gave way and I slid to the ground, shaking so hard that running away wasn't even an option. I was going to die. In an alley. In the dirt. Eaten by a *lion*.

"Oh please," I said, then squeezed my eyes closed. "Please, God, I don't want to die."

Not like this. Everything shut down; the breath rattled in my throat. I waited for the pain. The tearing.

A weird, wet sound and the cracking of bones made me look up, just in time to see Logan straighten from a crouch on the ground. Stark ass naked and swearing. He looked around, then found me. His expression softened and he held out a hand. "Natalia —"

I scrambled away, through the cold mud and ooze in the alley, but I didn't take my eyes off him. Some kind of trick. It had to be some kind of crazy fucking magic trick to put me off balance. He had a lot of money. He could pay someone for the special effects. This might all be some weird shit that billionaires did for fun, trying to scare me into staying with him. My throat wouldn't form sounds.

Logan took another step toward me. "Baby, listen to me. Just breathe. I can explain."

"Wh - wh - what..." I clutched my head, staggering to my feet with the help of the brick wall behind me. "I don't —"

"Hold on, just wait a second. I can explain."

The alley opened up behind me, only a few more feet until freedom, but he moved to the side, arms wide, and I froze. Logan's patient expression grew tense, a little hard. "Natalia, don't run. Please. Don't run."

"So you — you can kill me?" The words squeaked out, and I reached a shaking hand for the wall. My phone was in my purse, inside, and there was no way I could get inside with him in the way. Why didn't anyone come outside? Didn't they need more soup?

"I'll explain. Come inside." He gestured at the kitchen behind him, the broken door, but never took his eyes off me. Stalking one slow step at a time towards me, trapping me. Hunting me down.

I shook my head, sliding closer to the mouth of the alley. If I could get to the street, someone might help me. He was naked, after all, and a dead body lay cooling behind him. Someone would help me. "Get away from me."

"Baby —"

"I'm not your baby." It came out louder than I expected, and I clamped my lips together to keep from crying. I pointed at him with a shaking hand. "Get away from me. I don't know what the fuck is going on, but it's sick. *Sick.* You're messing with my head, and I never thought — I didn't think you would do that. So get the fuck away from me, and don't you ever, *ever* talk to me again."

"Natalia," he said, a sigh. Disappointed. "Let me explain."

I shook my head. "I'm done with your explanations."

When he opened his mouth to cajole me into staying and took another step towards me, I bolted. Turned and ran and fully expected him to leap at me, to chase me. Instead, only the sound of my panicked breathing followed me into the night.

chapter 11

When Logan heard her cursing someone in the alley, his lion burst out, and the rage and pain of the transformation hurled him through the metal door to confront the danger. And then he faced Natalia. She stared at him, terrified, and it shook him to his very core. He hated that she feared him. So he changed back.

And it didn't get better. It got worse.

She made a terrible keening sound and cringed smaller against the dirty bricks of the alley. He couldn't calm her, couldn't even get her to stay in the alley. When she turned and ran, he wanted to go after her but his clothes shredded in the change and he had nothing to wear. He dragged the manager's body behind the dumpster and retreated to the kitchen. He pulled on an apron and stayed out of sight, hoping none of the church-y volunteers caught sight of his nakedness around the food, and called Edgar.

Luckily, Edgar was still working near the restaurant and arrived with new clothes, a cleanup crew, and a lot of jokes within fifteen minutes. Logan changed quickly in one of the large SUVs as Edgar and his guys got rid of any evidence that the manager or anyone else had been in the alley. Logan took a few seconds to apologize to the volunteer coordinator inside the soup kitchen for himself and Natalia, blaming it on Natalia not feeling well. They were all very concerned, asking him over and over to pass their good wishes on to her, which just made him feel more like an ass. If only they really knew.

When he finally extricated himself from the circle of genteel older ladies, he found Edgar waiting on the sidewalk out front. His brother peered at his phone and said, "No sign of security cameras, which is good and bad. Good because there's no evidence against you, but bad because we can't tell which way your chef went."

"She just needs time." Logan stretched his shoulders; two quick changes like that always led to muscle aches, to feeling like his bones weren't connected right, but there was no way he ever would have chased Natalia down as a lion.

"Not too much time." Edgar glanced up from his phone with a frown. "Go get her, man."

"She's terrified. I'm not going to —"

"She saw you." Edgar said it slow and careful, like the problem was Logan not hearing clearly. "She knows what you are, what we all are. Now she's running around in the city. Logan, man, you have to get her somewhere safe until you can explain and make her understand."

He clenched his jaw, staring into the night where Natalia — bruised, scared, alone — wandered. Running away from the monster she thought he was. He'd killed Joey right in front of her without a second thought. Maybe he was a monster.

"I'm not going to hunt her down like some — gazelle. She'll come back when she's ready."

"No, she won't." Edgar sighed, ran a hand over his face until his expression resumed its neutral cast. "If you don't get her, Logan, I will."

A growl started in his chest, and Logan wrapped a fist in Edgar's shirt. "Do. Not. Touch her."

"Then go get your mate," his brother shot back. "It's your job, and you're not doing it."

"You didn't see her face." Logan turned away for a moment, glad the other vans and cars had disappeared, along with what remained of the shithead manager. Just his brother remained, and Logan didn't mind Edgar seeing him uncertain. Anyone else would have gotten thrown through a wall, but Edgar was the only person in the world he could tolerate knowing these things. "Edgar, she looked at me like — like —" He held his hands up, ashamed the nails were still dark and long. His lion remained too close to the surface, unhinged by the threat to his mate and her subsequent escape, the thought of her wandering the dark city alone made him want to burst through his skin again.

Edgar took a deep breath, holding his hands up. "Look, Logan. You're my brother and my leader. I say this with love and respect. Pull your head out of your ass, go catch your mate, and explain to her what the fuck is going on. If she starts screaming, wait until she stops and start talking again. Wash, rinse, repeat. She'll get it eventually."

"And if she doesn't? If she can't accept what we are?"

His expression hardened. "Then she wasn't really meant to be yours to begin with, was she?"

Logan tilted his head back to look at the stars, wishing he could see more through the light pollution of the city. He closed his eyes and tasted the air, trying to get a whiff of her. Nothing.

"Does she have her phone?" Edgar flipped at his phone, then frowned. Showed Logan a screen with blinking dots. "She's right here."

Logan held up her purse, retrieved from the kitchen. "She left her shit. You have a tracker in her phone?"

"I have a tracker for all of you, dumbass," Edgar said under his breath. "How the fuck else am I supposed to keep you all alive? Jesus. Okay, we do this the old fashioned way."

He got in the car, drove about half a block, then leaned out the window and gestured for Logan to get in. Logan looked at his brother, irritated. "What?"

"She's at O'Shea's."

Logan's scowl darkened. "How do you know that?"

Edgar's gaze fixed straight ahead. "Ruby owes me a favor."

Ruby. Logan got in the car without a word, though he wanted to put his fist through the windshield. "She knows Ruby and Rafe."

"Oh yes."

From the grim sound of it, Logan didn't want to hear the rest of the story. He rubbed his temples and tried to figure out what the hell he would tell Natalia when he found her, how he could possibly explain. Shapeshifters. Lions. Abrupt violence as a normal part of the world. Particularly when her friends, wolf shifters, got involved. He pinched the bridge of his nose. So maybe they wouldn't be moving in together this weekend after all.

chapter 12

I wandered aimlessly, not seeing the street signs I passed, but eventually buildings looked familiar. People filled the streets, looking at me askance as I staggered along. My brain clicked slowly, the world moving past in flickers and flashes instead of a rolling film. I couldn't stop the trembling that wracked me from head to toe. Nothing worked right.

The sign for O'Shea's drew me in, dragged me across a street and through traffic. I didn't hear the honking. I hit the door and almost crashed into Rafe, lurking near the door. He caught me by the shoulders, expression strange. "Nat. What's —" His head tilted and he inhaled deeply near me, then held me at arm's length to study me. He pulled at the collar of my shirt, exposing my neck and shoulder, and I tried to push him away. Rafe made a strange sound in his throat, then turned and walked me into the bar. He steered me to a stool at the very end, nearest the office he shared with Ruby. He poured whiskey into a glass, three or four shots worth, and put it in front of me. "Down the hatch."

"I don't think that's —" My voice came out all wobbly and uncertain, and his frown deepened.

"You look like someone just walked over your grave. Put it down, Nat."

So I did, and the whiskey landed like a rock in my stomach. A warm, sloshy rock. It took the edge off... whatever it was I felt. For a moment, a hysterical giggle fought to escape my throat and I gripped the edge of the bar, holding on to it and my sanity by the tips of my fingers alone. Rafe splashed more amber liquid into the glass. "Again."

"I haven't eaten all day, Rafe."

"Good." His gaze moved past me, to the door, and I froze. Terrified. Thinking a demon lion would burst through the door and murder me. He looked back at me, and his head tilted in a decidedly nonhuman fashion. "You're safe here, Nat. Believe me."

"I d-don't know what you're talking about."

The next shot of whiskey seemed less like a bad idea, more like stress management. Seeing a lion turn into a man — and a man I'd been kissing only minutes before — deserved a bit of liquid courage.

Rafe waved away a friend who tried to get his attention, and leaned forward with his elbows on the bar. His voice lowered, a shared secret. "You smell a lot like Logan Chase. Did he do something to you, Nat?"

"He saved me," I said to the glass of whiskey, trying to hide the words in the fragrant liquor that stung my nostrils. "And then he — he — turned into something terrible. Something horrible."

"What did he turn into?"

"You won't believe me." I laughed, surprised at how much it hurt to admit. "Because it isn't possible."

"I will. And it is."

I lifted my gaze to his, surprised that his normally gray eyes were suddenly almost gold. For one crazy moment, I decided to believe him. To trust him. The words slipped out before I could change my mind. "He turned into a lion. Killed the man who attacked me. And turned back into a man."

I waited for the laughter or the call to the loony bin. A 72-hour hold at City General. Instead, Rafe nodded, gave me a bigger drink, and said, "I'll call Ruby. Just stay here."

So I sat and nursed the drink, though I wanted to pound the entire bottle until it dulled the pain and fear. All the promise of that relationship with Logan disappeared in a flash. In less than a heartbeat. Imagine — turning into a lion.

My forehead connected to the bar with a thud. The shivers didn't shop jostling me on the stool. I couldn't control as my fingers trembled around the glass. I didn't even have my purse. It still sat in the soup kitchen. Ruby didn't ask me any questions when she appeared in front of me, instead only holding my hands between hers to try to warm the chill from them. It didn't work, but it helped me feel less alone in the world.

Yet Rafe hadn't been particularly surprised by what I said. And he thought I smelled like Logan. We'd been spending a lot of time together, sure, but it wasn't like I used his detergent or worc his cologne or anything. I looked at my friend, desperate for other reassurances. "Am I crazy?"

"No, babe." The silver ring spun in her lip as she worried it with her tongue, a nervous habit when she was very angry or very upset. She rubbed my shoulder, leaning on the bar very much like her brother. "It's just a bit of a shock."

"He turned into a lion," I whispered, to make sure she knew the kind of crazy she dealt with. This wasn't the garden variety hallucination. This was semi-pro. Maybe Olympic quality.

She took a deep breath, then nodded. "I know. Rafe told me." She picked up my hands again, studied my fingers and then my wrists. "I haven't seen you in a couple of days. Can you go back and tell me what happened?"

It took forever to unravel the past few days in my mind, trying to rewind to the last time I'd seen her through the blur of so many hours of what I'd thought was happiness. I fumbled the glass, feeling uncoordinated and disjointed. "Joey attacked me at the restaurant... ten, twelve days ago? Logan's brothers saved me. Logan saved me. He protected me, took me home, took care of me. Asked me to live with him."

She concentrated on wiping another glass clean, the spotless white towel working the same part of the glass over and over and over again. Her voice remained carefully neutral. "Seems awful fast, Nat."

"I know." I stared at the lines of liquor bottles behind her. "Really fast. But it felt right. It felt good. I felt safe with him, protected. We were looking for an apartment, and I took a few days off work to recover from what Joey — did. He came with me to help tonight at the soup kitchen. I took out the trash, and Joey was there. He attacked me again and then —" I cut off, struggled to breathe. She pressed the full glass of whiskey into my hand, and I gulped it down mechanically. It eased the words from around the lump in my throat. "The door was locked but he went through it. He flew through it, but he was a lion. An enormous fucking lion. He — I think he killed Joey, I don't know. He just lay there. And then Logan stood up where the lion used to be, and he was naked, and he said he wanted to explain."

"Did he? Explain?" Still quiet and reserved, as if I hadn't just told her my sort-of boyfriend turned into a lion.

I looked at her blankly. "I ran. Are you kidding? I fucking ran. What is there to explain? He's a monster. Or a total prick, if this is some kind of joke."

"I don't think it's a joke, Nat." Ruby returned to cleaning her glass, watching it instead of me. "You should let him explain. Make a decision after you've had a chance to calm down, hear what he has to say."

"What could he possibly say?" The words exploded out of me as I stared at her in disbelief. "What is there to possibly say?"

She shrugged, tipped a little more liquor into my glass, and then canted her head at the swinging door to the kitchen. "I'll grab you some snacks, Nat. Rafe said you hadn't eaten."

She fiddled with her phone as she walked away, and I rested my forehead against my arms on the bar. Un-fucking-believable.

The whiskey softened the world, eased the panic, stole away the fear until I leaned against the bar and tried desperately just to stay upright. I wanted to go home and sleep, to wake up from all of this and realize that everything had been a dream — every bit of it, from the night I met Logan to the moment he killed Joey. I just prayed he would leave me alone. Nothing else about him said half-measures were possible, but he'd been respectful enough to that point that I hoped a simple "get the fuck out of my life" would suffice. If not — well. I could hide somewhere. Run away. Until I had to go to work and he was there.

I closed my eyes and put my face in my hands. God help me.

A warm hand landed on my shoulder, and I knew it a flash it was Logan. I didn't even have to look to know it was him by the way he displaced air, how power and strength filled the room when he entered it. I cleared my throat and managed to say, "Are you going to kill me now?"

A long pause. Then something like a sigh. "I could. But then who would make me soufflé when I want it?"

He was teasing me, and this wasn't a joking matter. I lifted myself up enough to push the glass of whiskey, magically full again, away, and glared at him. "I wish I'd never met you."

The world swirled and wobbled around me, and time skipped. It might have been an hour or only a deep breath before he said, voice low and pained, "Don't say that. Don't ever say that. Please."

Tears burned my eyes and I didn't know why. Because I was afraid or sad or tired or just disappointed, because he'd been so perfect, so wonderful, and it was all a facade. He was just another lying douchebag. His secrets were even worse than the normal douchebags, who were only married or had kids or used drugs.

"Please don't cry." Logan's voice broke and then he moved, crushed me against his chest. "Don't ever cry because of me."

"I want you to leave," I said, choking on the words. "I want you to go away."

"Let me explain," he said. His cheek rubbed the top of my head, and he pulled me closer. "Give me a chance to explain."

"Let her go."

The deep voice hit me like a bucket of cold water. Rafe. I looked up and tried to focus as he doubled and then tripled in my vision. But Ruby and her brother both stood there, facing off with Logan. And Logan somehow expanded, that rumble in his chest again but not cute and warm like when he did it around me. This was threatening. Rafe didn't blink, pointing at the stool I'd occupied. "Put her down, feline."

"You don't get to order me around, Rafe." Logan still held me securely, didn't seem inclined to release me, and from the corner of my eye I saw a blurry figure that could have been Edgar. "She's mine."

"She was ours first," Ruby said. Folded her arms over her chest. "And this is our den, and it's full of pack tonight, so you and your friend probably won't make it out without a few scars. Put her back on that stool and take your own. If you want to explain something, do it here — but touch her again and I'll put you in the hospital."

Logan growled; there was no other word for it, though snarl would have worked. He put me back on the stool and occupied the one next to me, but he wasn't happy about it. Ruby scowled at him, still cleaning her glass, and pointed at me. "Start explaining."

Another snarl. He took my hand, laced our fingers together. When I looked at him, his eyes shone gold, lit from within. My heart stopped, because they were the lion's eyes, staring at me. Consuming me.

chapter 13

Logan nearly took the door off the hinges when he saw Natalia slumped against the bar inside. As it was, he launched a drunk who got in his way back ten feet. Then he was close enough to her to touch her, to inhale her, but he held back. He didn't ever want to see terror in her face again, ever. Especially when he caused that fear.

He held her hand as it trembled and shook, and concentrated on keeping his voice low and steady. Calm. Willing her to relax. She was drunk as hell, staring at him wide-eyed and wobbly. Logan took a deep breath and held her gaze. "Baby, listen to me. I would never, ever hurt you. Ever."

Her chin trembled.

He couldn't help it, touched her cheek. Adored the softness of her skin against his fingers. Wanted to pull her against his chest and inhale her, carry her away and take care of her. Logan took a deep breath. "What you saw tonight, Natalia, I'm not proud of. I should not have lost control like that. I frightened you, and I'm very sorry."

She didn't pull away, at least. She blinked rapidly, searching his face for something. Natalia whispered, "Tell me it was a joke. A trick. Some mirrors or a projector or something."

"I wish I could." Logan sighed and rested his forehead against hers. "But it isn't a trick, my darling. It's who I am."

"It can't be." Her voice broke. "It's not fair."

Logan closed his eyes, holding her face gently and stroking his thumbs across her cheeks. "It isn't all bad."

She drew back, wiping under her eyes, and his heart sank to see the tears streaking her face. Natalia took a deep breath, though she hiccupped and nearly fell off her stool. "Can you do it whenever you want? Or just when you're angry?"

"I control it." Usually, he wanted to add, but any caveats at that point could have set her off. "I can show you if you want. Just not here."

She flinched, holding onto the bar. "No thank you."

Logan almost laughed, rubbing his forehead. He looked up as something bumped his elbow — a glass of liquor. Ruby still frowned at him, but Rafe looked more sympathetic. Logan took a deep breath and raised the glass in a toast, "Thanks," before he drained it. The liquid courage helped.

"So are you magic?"

He snorted, almost spat the liquor back in her face. He coughed, pounding his chest before he looked at her, and croaked, "What?"

"It has to be magic." She looked so earnest and confused, the urge to kiss her nearly overwhelmed Logan. Natalia looked at the ceiling, struggling to order her thoughts as she gestured widely. "That's — otherwise it doesn't make any sense. It has to be magic. Or — or God, maybe? Are you an angel?"

Rafe laughed and walked away. Ruby didn't even crack a smile, her arms folded over her chest. Logan cleared his throat and tried not to laugh at Natalia's questions. "No, baby, I'm not an angel, and I'm not magic. Some people are born like this, but it's possible for normal humans to be changed. It spreads like a virus if there are very specific conditions."

"Oh my." Natalia fell off her stool.

Logan jumped up to help her, wanting to laugh more, and carefully propped her back up. She braced against his chest and stared up at him with eyes round as saucers. "Did you infect me?"

"No, Natalia." Logan pressed his nose to her hair, closing his eyes as he drank her in. He didn't want to even consider it, but it might be the last time she let him touch her. "It takes a deep bite to change someone. Touching, kissing, sex — none of that does it. Just a bite."

"Does it hurt?"

"If I were to bite you? I've never —"

"No, when you do ... that. When you're the other thing. It sounded like breaking bones. Does it hurt?"

"A little." He pressed his lips to her forehead. "You get used to it, though. It's a small price to pay."

"Oh." She frowned at his chest, then sighed. "I'm really tired. I want to go home."

"Come home with me," Logan murmured, touching her cheek again. "Come home with me so I can take care of you."

"You're too scary." Natalia poked his chest, trying to look fierce. "And I don't like cats."

He laughed, rubbing his temples. Shit. "You don't like cats?"

"No." Natalia folded her arms over her chest. "They're judgey."

"She's a dog person," Ruby said, leaning forward on the bar and fixing Logan with a grim look. "And will stay that way. Understood?"

Logan took a deep breath as he faced the female alpha of the BloodMoon pack, but he wasn't about to let Ruby intimidate him into giving up Natalia. "She makes her own decisions, Ruby Leigh."

"Ruby Leigh?" Natalia giggled, then clapped a hand over her mouth and looked aghast. "I'm so sorry I laughed. That's a beautiful name."

Ruby gave her a sideways look but saved her ire for Logan. "Look, cat. She's under my protection, got it? She calls and says 'come help me,' and you're going to have twenty pissed off wolves at your door. Literally. And then we will pull every single contract and deal we have with you, and so will every other pack in this half of the country. If you hurt her, we will ruin you. And then we'll kill you."

Logan believed every word she said. And since the packs made up about a third of his revenue, it wasn't an idle threat. He could recover financially, but the damage to his heart and his lion from losing Natalia would be irreparable. Natalia hiccupped again, then leaned toward her friend and whispered, "You have wolves?"

"Honey," Ruby said, sparing the chef a patient look. "We *are* wolves."

"No. Way." Natalia's eyes widened, and she pushed back from the bar. "You're fucking kidding —" And promptly toppled off the stool once more.

Logan picked her up and said under his breath, "Your friend needs to get chairs instead of bar stools, doesn't she?"

"Don't make fun of me," Natalia said.

"Never," he said, and kissed her temple. "Never ever. Now tell Ruby you want to come home with me, and we'll get out of here."

Natalia took a deep breath, frowning as she stared at the smooth, unmarked surface of the bar. "I want to lay down. And you have my bag. And my phone."

"Edgar has it right here," he said. He gestured, and his brother approached, placing the bag on the bar next to her elbow and winking when Natalia looked up at him.

She beamed at him, "Edgar!" and threw her arms around his neck.

Logan looked at Ruby, a bit astonished, and the wolf shook her head with a long-suffering sigh. "She's a happy drunk. A very friendly, very happy drunk. No filter."

As if on cue, Natalia grabbed Edgar's face and mushed the skin on his cheeks. Her whisper was loud as a shout even in the busy bar. "Are you a cat too? Are you a magic cat?"

"I'm a lion," Edgar said, though he struggled to keep his face composed and neutral. "Not a cat. King of the jungle, got it?"

Still poking Edgar's cheeks, she looked over her shoulder at Ruby. "*Lions*, Ruby. Lions!"

"Okay," Logan said, and looped his arm around Natalia's waist. "Before she tells the entire city, we're going to go. I will protect her, wolf."

"See that you do." Ruby eyed Edgar askance, then pointed a scarlet-painted talon at him. "I hold you personally responsible, Edgar Chase."

"She's his mate," Edgar said, and Logan punched his shoulder. Edgar ignored him to fiddle with his phone instead. "Don't deny it, Logan. She is. She's yours. Just don't mess it up now." He looked up and nodded to Ruby. "We'll be in touch with you and Rafe to discuss any necessary ... arrangements."

Logan supported Natalia as she wobbled and stared up at him. "What did he say?"

"Nothing, baby." Logan kissed her and readjusted his grip on her waist. He looked at Ruby. "I'll have her call you tomorrow. You might have some explaining to do, too."

She smiled, though, and shrugged as she turned away. "Right. Good luck."

Logan half-carried Natalia to the SUV and settled her in the backseat next to him as Edgar got in the driver's seat. He stroked her cheek, "Natalia, if—"

A quiet snore was her only answer. Logan laughed and tilted his head back, rubbing his forehead as he closed his eyes. The pain of the change faded somewhat, aided by the drink Rafe gave him, but he wanted only to crawl into bed and sleep a solid ten hours. First he had to make sure Natalia was cared for. The SUV rolled to a stop, and Logan looked up. "This isn't home."

"No, this is her home." Edgar didn't turn around. "If you take her to the mansion, she'll feel trapped. Take her here and give her the option of kicking you out."

"When did you get so smart?" Logan kicked his door open and tried to wake Natalia up, but she made a face and pushed him away with a muttered, "Bad kitty."

Edgar sighed, glancing at his phone once more. "I've always been this smart, you just never listened before. Kitty."

"Fuck off." Logan lifted Natalia out of the car, throwing her over his shoulder so if she puked it wouldn't end up all over him. "But thank you."

Edgar raised his hand in a dismissive wave, and drove off as soon as the door closed. Logan carried her up the stairs to the shitty apartment, wishing he hadn't been quite so picky about the new one. At least then he could have taken her back to a place they both belonged. Soon, though. Soon he would take her home.

chapter 14

I woke in a fog. Forcing my eyes open only made the room spin, so I closed them and pulled the sheets over my head. I still felt drunk. A moan escaped.

"Drink."

The soft voice made me freeze, my stomach clenching in fear. I almost couldn't pull the sheets down from my face to peek at whoever stood over me. Logan. He looked apprehensive, but held out a bottle of water. "You should drink some water. You'll feel better."

"I'm never going to feel better," I groaned, and covered my face again. Too much sunlight sent daggers through my eyes to my brain. The night came back in flashes — sitting at Ruby's bar, pounding whiskey like it was my job.

He sat on the mattress next to me and nudged my side. "Seriously, Natalia."

I groaned and grumbled, but I knew he was right. I sat up, waiting for the room to stop spinning before reaching for the cold bottle. Maybe hair of the dog was better than just water, but anything that smelled like alcohol might push me over the edge. I sipped carefully, drawing my knees up to my chest. I wore only a t-shirt and panties, and his gaze drifted to my bare thighs. I blushed, looking away. "What happened?"

Logan took a deep breath, leaning back against a pillow along the foot of the bed. I studied him carefully — given the choice, he always stayed close to me, touching me. To distance himself like that meant something was wrong. I rubbed my forehead.

He looked tense as a coiled spring. "Do you remember what happened at the soup kitchen?"

I squinted, finishing off the bottle of water. It came back in pieces. Him chopping fruit after he burned the chili. Talking about moving in. Taking the trash out. And then — "Joey," I said.

"Yes."

I sucked in a breath, staring at him as I backed up against the headboard. "And you — you were —"

"A lion." Logan nodded but otherwise didn't move. "I was a lion. We talked about it a little at Ruby's bar, if you remember."

The empty water bottle fell to the floor and rolled under the bed. I put my hands over my face as the sickness welled up in my stomach. It wouldn't stop in my head, the image of the lion landing on Joey, the red across his chest and the ground, the dull crunches as Logan stood up out of the body of the lion.

"Breathe," he murmured, soft and slow. "Just breathe through your nose."

"What the fuck are you?" I couldn't look at him. The flaking walls of my tiny studio closed in around me. Like a cage. A trap.

"A shapeshifter. I'm a lion. There are others — wolves, bears, hyenas. Most predators."

I shook my head, but his words jogged something else loose. Wolves. I stared at him, struggling to breathe. "Ruby and Rafe — they're?"

"Wolf shifters," he said, nodding. As if this were a perfectly normal conversation to be having. That my best friend and her brother, who I'd known for years, practically since I left foster care, were werewolves. But he went on, slow and deliberate. "They're the alphas of their pack. Fierce leaders. Very protective." Logan smiled a little ruefully. "Very protective of you, too. They threatened to kill me yesterday if I wasn't a perfect gentleman."

"Oh. That's nice," I said in a weak voice. None of this made sense. "How - how many are there? Of y-your kind?"

"Of lions?" He frowned in thought, staring up at the ceiling, and I refused to admit it was the most adorable expression his face could wear. "Not many. My brothers and I are one pride. There are two more prides in other parts of the country, but there are very few of us. Less than fifty total, I'd say."

My stomach burbled in warning. I slid to the edge of the bed. "I need to excuse myself for a moment."

He didn't move but only nodded, watching me with those golden eyes.

I didn't wait for any other response and hustled to the bathroom, where I threw up pretty much everything I'd ever eaten and half a bottle of whiskey. Holy shit. I sat on the edge of the tub and covered my eyes, fumbling for a washcloth so I could wipe the tears and snot and yuck off my face. The tears wouldn't stop, though, even after my stomach remained in place. Cold water on my face didn't help, yelling at myself in my head to get my shit together didn't work, nothing would stop the tears. So I gave up waiting for them to stop, brushed my teeth, and walked back out to confront Logan.

He still lay draped across the end of my bed, looking more like a cat than I could have admitted the day before.

I put my hands on my hips and fixed him with my fiercest look. "Okay. Start explaining."

Logan sat up and rested his elbows on his knees. "I like you, Natalia."

I snorted, about to turn away, but his quiet words near knocked me flat. "Really. I love you. I love you, Natalia. I've loved you since you kicked me out of your restaurant."

I flushed, but I couldn't look away from his fiery, glowing, beautiful eyes.

He went on, almost hypnotic in the measured rhythm of his words. "Our kind, we recognize our partners right away. You're meant to be mine. But you're not a shifter, so it's possible I'm not meant to be yours. I will spend my entire life showing you that we belong together. I will do anything to show you now. I love you. I want you to be my mate, to be my family."

The breath caught in my throat, my lungs constricted until the world grew dark around the edges. Mate? Family?

The words dragged out of me. "You mean — what do you mean?"

A smile tugged at the corner of his mouth. Logan eased to his feet. Took a slow step toward me, his hands held out in invitation. Ready to draw me close to him, to hug me, hold me. "I love you, Natalia. That's what I mean. I want to marry you, to take you as my mate. If you want to become a lion, I could change you. But you don't have to — I love you as you are. I love you exactly like this."

I pressed the heels of my hands against my forehead, staring at him. The headache pounded against my eyes. Become a lion? Become a monster like the one that killed Joey? Uncontrolled and uncontrollable? I swallowed hard, then turned and strode into the kitchen for more water. I braced my hands on the flimsy kitchen island. "Change."

His eyebrows arched. "You want me to change?"

"Yes." I gulped water and wiped my mouth with a shaking hand. "I want to see it. You want me to be near you. I need to see what you — what you are."

"Okay. Just — remember to breathe, Natalia." He never took his eyes off me as he stripped down, pulling his clothes off without a hint of modesty. He even folded them carefully before placing them on my bed. I refused to be distracted by the hard lines of muscle across his abdomen, the straps of muscle over his hip and down to his — I jerked my eyes back to his face, my cheeks burning, and found him grinning.

Logan took a deep breath, making fists in front of himself before flexing his shoulders and chest, and then... His skin tore open. Bursts of red and white and yellow as he turned inside out. Bones cracked and tendons popped. A scream caught in my throat and I couldn't move, every muscle frozen. Holy shit. Holy fucking shit.

A lion stood in my living room, in my apartment. He was easily five feet tall at the shoulders, his massive maned head at eye level with me. Warm golden eyes studied me, more intelligent than predatory, and his coat looked like velvet. Massive paws, larger than the dinner plates at the restaurant, tread silently over the stained carpet as he flowed a few feet closer to me. I backed up until I bumped into the fridge, and one of my magnets fell off, shattering as it hit the cracked linoleum.

He made a huffing noise, somewhere between a chirp and a purr, and I held my arms across my chest, trying to breathe through the panic. The reasonable part of my brain tried to explain that it was him, it was Logan, and he would never hurt me, but the caveman part of my brain said to run the fuck away. Fast.

A pink tongue lolled out of his mouth, but the finger-length teeth remained mostly hidden. He grumbled and huffed again, getting closer still. I forced myself to stay where I was even as he eased into the kitchen and bumped his head against me. Almost knocked me right over. I reached out to steady myself, and my fingers sank into his mane. Deep and wiry, a thick mass of hair that covered halfway to his shoulders. Mostly golden, but it had a few streaks of black in it. My hands tightened to fists, grabbing more of his mane, and he shifted his paws. I tried to release him, to back away, but he rubbed his face against my middle with another cat noise. Then — the rumble started.

My heart dropped because it sounded a little too much like a growl, but as I stood there, pinned between the fridge and a lion, it bounced through me. A purr. A real freaking purr, the more substantial cousin of that cute grumble when he was in his human body. I put a hand over my eyes. His human body.

Logan purred louder and his wide pink tongue rasped against my thigh. My face burned, and I backed up. "Don't you dare."

I could have sworn that lion laughed at me and licked my knee. The purr grew louder. I held my breath as he stalked me around the island, his head lowering and the intensity of his gaze increasing along with the purr. It rattled through my brain and almost drove away the headache, until I bumped into the bed and fell backward across the mattress.

Logan the lion placed a giant paw on the mattress next to my hip, raising himself up to look down at me. Then his giant face lowered and he licked from my throat to the top of my cheek. I spluttered and turned away. "Enough. Enough."

Before I could look at him, the popping and tearing erupted behind me and then naked Logan — human once more — flopped onto the bed next to me. I rolled away but he didn't follow, his expression pained as he lay there in silence.

"It hurts, doesn't it?"

Only his harsh breathing answered, and a low groan as his hands clenched.

He lay there, eyes closed, and for the first time, I had the chance to study him. Taut muscles along his shoulders and chest looked like they came from manual labor, not a fancy gym, but scars decorated his torso as well. A hard life led to scars like that. A light smattering of fur across his chest tapered to a narrow trail from his stomach to the nest of curls above his cock, impressive even while soft. I held my breath and bit my lip. The urge to touch him, to run my hands all over him, almost overwhelmed me.

As if he could read my thoughts, his cock twitched. Grew. A massive hard-on stood up against his stomach, made him look like a Greek hero in repose across my bed. My heart raced. Logan didn't open his eyes, his voice low and throaty. "I can feel you looking at me. If you want to touch me — please. Go ahead. I'm yours."

"I thought you said it hurt," I said, barely a whisper. Not believing I actually considered running my hands over his chest, down his washboard abs, up his cock to the perfect head where a single drop of liquid formed.

"It hurts more that you're not touching me," he murmured, his hand sliding over the sheets to squeeze my knee. "Natalia, I've dreamed of you touching me. Please."

My breath came faster but I wasn't quite brave enough to just reach out for his junk. Instead, I picked up his hand and examined his fingers, amazed they'd been paws and claws only a few moments before. My fingers traced the veins and muscles up his forearm and around his bicep, across his chest. I ran my nails across his shoulders, and a smile twitched across his face. But otherwise he didn't move.

I bit my lip, easing closer so I could see as his nipples tightened. My breath against his chest made him jump, and his fists tightened in the sheets, but his face remained perfectly relaxed. I licked his nipple and he groaned. It seemed a strange reversal that only a few moments before he could have torn me to pieces, and yet he lay on my bed and didn't move as I nibbled across his chest and watched the muscles tighten in his thighs. My palms stroked across his stomach, along his hips and down to his thighs, though his hips lifted off the mattress when I avoided his junk. But still he didn't touch me, waiting.

"I don't understand this," I said. My heart raced, desire coursed through me, and I wanted to tear off my underwear and straddle him. Ride him until I came and he came and we made a disaster of the bed. Put the headboard through the shitty plaster on the wall. Made the neighbors think the floor would collapse down on them. I shook my head, drifting my hands back up to his stomach so I could count the ripples of his abs. "You're you, and then you're that —

other thing, and then back to this. Perfect. Whole. How does that even work? I don't understand."

"I know it's strange." His voice came out strangled, and his hips lifted again in a slow thrust. "Maybe it is magic. It sometimes feels like magic."

I bit back a laugh, getting more than a little pleasure out of tormenting him like this. I'd spent enough time off-balance and uncertain around him, and now I had him — literally — in the palm of my hand. I leaned down and breathed against his cock, the heated flesh twitching. He groaned. I wrapped my hand around the base, my fingers still a good inch apart despite squeezing, and stroked slowly to the head.

His breath escaped in a rush and Logan rubbed my thigh, his eyes still closed. He kneaded my leg with his strong fingers, and I had to swallow an indecent noise. Holy Christ.

"Keep going," he breathed, making progress up my thigh. I shifted and squeezed my legs together as I knelt next to him, and his hand drifted up my thigh to my butt.

I closed my eyes and stroked him again, then licked the tip in a slow drag that had his fingers digging into my ass. I rocked forward, took him in my mouth and ran my tongue around the spongy flesh. He tasted salty and musky and — different. Wilder. He worked my ass with one hand, his other hand rising slowly to rest on his stomach, just above where my hand held him.

Logan took a shaky breath. "I love you, Natalia."

"Tell me," I started, and then sighed in anticipation as his fingers slid under my panties, dipped under my thighs toward where I ached to feel him. I licked the underside of his cock, wanting to take more of him but needing to hear his voice. "Tell me how a lion would do this."

He laughed, fingers bolder in their explorations, and his voice deepened considerably. "The lion would have you on your knees already."

I wiggled, spreading my thighs so he had easier access to trace slow circles through my sex. "Well, technically I am on my knees."

A smile, slow and lazy, spread across his face but still he kept his eyes closed. He pressed a finger inside me and I gasped, back arching. Logan groaned, his other hand resting on the back of my head. "I love the sounds you make, Natalia. Do it again."

And I did, as he added another finger deep inside and his thumb pressed against my clit. I took his cock in my mouth again, deeper, sucking more as I tried not to moan and press back against his hand. Logan's hand tightened in my hair, guided me to take more of him. "The lion wants you on your hands and knees, your ass in the air. Wants to bite your shoulder to hold you in place while we fuck you. Drive into you until we mark you, until you're ours all the way through."

He kept talking and I kept moving, stroking him with my hand as I sucked the head and rocked my hips against his hand. Logan groaned, deep and loud, and when I looked up, I found him watching me with those brilliant gold eyes.

His hips thrust against my face, and his fingers worked faster, circling and pushing and driving me closer and closer to the edge of pure ecstasy. I cried out, freezing as my muscles contracted in waves around his fingers, trying to draw them deeper, and Logan's hand tightened in my hair, pulled my face forcefully against his stomach.

I was lost. Pure pleasure rolled through me as he took control, holding me carefully as his hips thrust, and then he cursed. His cock jerked, and a heated rush of thick fluid coated my tongue, filled my mouth. My thighs tightened against his wrist as Logan continued stroking me, teasing and tormenting, and I moaned.

Logan moved to his side and pulled me up so my head rested against his chest, and he pulled me close against him. He smelled like sweat and sex, and so did I. I closed my eyes as he wrapped his arms around me, rubbing my back. He kissed behind my ear, along my jaw. "You are perfect, Natalia."

I didn't want to think about anything, certainly not the real world that waited outside my apartment. We were different. Too different. Even if I felt an unbelievable connection to him, even if the world only felt right when I was in his arms — I didn't want to live in the same world, where wolves threatened him and he killed a man in an alley without apparent consequences. I squeezed my eyes shut and held him close, tracing his shoulder blades with my fingers so I would remember what they felt like when I no longer had him to hold on to.

Logan rumbled his contentment and managed to pull a sheet over us, and then lay on his back and pulled me onto his chest. His heart beat steadily against my ear. He nibbled along my shoulder. "Say something, baby."

Tears burned my sinuses as I hid my face against his neck. Almost hoped he wouldn't hear as I said, "I love you."

Silence. Logan took a deep breath. "I hear a 'but' following that."

"But I don't think I can do this." Tears fell against his neck. His hands stilled, fell to the mattress at his sides.

"Why not?" Painfully controlled, careful. As if I told him I didn't like bread.

"I just need to think." It was a coward's way out, hedging. And we both knew it. "It's too much changing too fast. I barely knew you a week ago, and now — now there's lions and wolves and shit, and people dying in alleys, and moving apartments. I just — I need time to think and figure this out."

Logan didn't speak for a long, long time.

chapter 15

He'd been shot once with a high-powered rifle. It hurt less than Natalia saying she didn't want to be with him.

Logan stayed until she cried herself out and fell asleep, then shifted her off his chest and got dressed. Walked out of the apartment in a fog and headed down the street. He didn't remember calling Edgar, but he blinked and one of the dark sedans pulled up next to him, Benedict at the wheel.

He got in the car and stared straight ahead, unable to look at his brother lest his face crack and fall to pieces. "Don't say a word."

The lawyer looked at him for a long time, then sighed and pulled into traffic. Neither of them spoke until Benedict parked in front of the mansion, kept his hands on the steering wheel and looked down at the gearshift between them. "I'm sorry, brother."

Logan threw open the car door and strode into the house, slamming the door behind him.

Sorry didn't cover it.

For the first few days after he left her apartment, Logan's lion raged. Roared and paced in his head, desperate to get their mate back. Desperate to smell her, to touch her. To feed her and hold her at night. But she wasn't there. He couldn't go to her. She didn't want them. Didn't want *him*.

It hurt with a deep burn that gutted him unexpectedly throughout the day. He would be fine, in the middle of a meeting to acquire a new business or negotiate a new trade deal, and he would think of her blue eyes laughing at him, or the way she bit her lip when he touched her, or the scent of her shampoo all over his chest. And his heart would seize up, and the lion would rage to the surface, and he would have to excuse himself before he tore every person in the room into bloody scraps.

Benedict or Atticus would find him, drag him down to the gym, and make him lift weights or box until he was exhausted. Then he would drop face-first onto his bed — his empty, lonely fucking bed — and sleep until he had to get up again.

They still owned the restaurant. He couldn't bring himself to sell it. It was a cash cow, once Carter and Benedict finally straightened out the books. In fact, it was more profitable than several of his other ventures, so Benedict started looking into other restaurants to purchase and rehab. Carter managed the day-to-day at Natalia's restaurant, and though he gave regular updates to Benedict and Atticus, he said nothing to Logan.

And that was just fine with Logan.

He didn't want to know how she was. He didn't want to hear she'd moved on. Not knowing hurt less than knowing she loved someone else.

Two weeks passed, then three. Then a month. And still he could not bring himself to care about anything.

Logan sat in his office, staring out the window at the city. Not thinking. He did a lot of that, after Natalia. Just not thinking about anything. That way nothing would remind him of her smile or the curl in her hair.

The door opened and closed behind him, and Logan turned to confront whoever dared disturb him. He'd left strict instructions with his executive assistant that no one ... "Edgar. What do you want?"

His brother walked up and planted his fists on Logan's desk, leaning forward in a posture so aggressive that Logan sat back in surprise. Edgar's eyes blazed a kaleidoscope of golds and reds as he gritted words out between his teeth. "I'm done with this pouting bullshit. Pull your head out of your ass before I challenge you for alpha."

"Watch your mouth or I will beat the shit out of you," Logan snapped, sitting up.

"Do it. Go ahead. I'll even wait for you to hike up your big girl panties."

"Fuck. Off." Logan snarled, lurching to his feet to loom over Edgar. "I will throw you out this fucking window, lion."

Edgar squared off with him, practically bumping chests. "Stop moping around, you shithead, and go get your girl."

"She doesn't want me." The words hurt too much to say quietly. Instead they burst forth with enough volume to throw Edgar back a few steps. Logan followed, slamming his fists into Edgar's chest. "Don't you get it? She doesn't want us. We asked her and she said no. It's over."

"She said she had to fucking think, dumbass!" Edgar hit him back. "That's not a 'no.' That's not a 'never.' That's a 'not yet.'"

Logan picked up a chair and threw it into the wall, roaring. "You didn't hear her. You didn't see her face. It was a 'never.' And fuck you for bringing it up."

"I talked to Ruby," Edgar said. Ducked as Logan threw another chair, this time directly at him. He retreated but kept talking, hands turning dark as the nails grew into claws. "Natalia is miserable. She wants to talk to you but she can't. She doesn't understand any of this, but she's trying to."

"I told you — I *ordered* you not to talk to her." Logan ran out of chairs, blinded by rage and pain, and reached for the coffee table near the fireplace instead. It shattered in a cascade of glass against the wall a second after Edgar leapt to the side. Logan snarled again, his teeth growing too large and sharp to speak. "I fucking *told you* —"

"I talked to *Ruby*," Edgar repeated. He held up his hands. "She called me. The pack is ready to come after you because Natalia is a mess. She won't tell them what you did or what happened, but Rafe is about a week shy of knocking on our door. You have to fix this, Logan."

"How am I supposed to fix it?" The rage simmered but dissipated, until nothing remained by hurt and exhaustion. He rubbed his face, bending to brace his hands on his knees. "Damn it, Edgar. She doesn't want me."

"She was scared and confused and hungover." His brother approached slowly. "You can win her back."

Logan faced his brother, felt himself balancing on a knife's edge. "If she rejects me again, Edgar, it'll kill me. Or you'll have to kill me, because the lion will take over and I'll be gone."

"I've got a plan, brother." Edgar looked around for a chair and found only kindling and twisted metal. He scowled at his brother. "Now where the fuck do I sit?"

"Sit on the fucking floor, dick. You're the one who ran in here and pissed me off." Logan returned to his desk and gave his trashcan a kick for good measure. A spark of hope kindled in his heart for the first time in a month.

chapter 16

I didn't want to go, but Benedict called and said he needed my input on a new business plan. He wanted to expand to a second restaurant and needed recommendations for how to write the proposal. I shook my head and almost turned around for the fifth time as my car rattled up to the gate at the mansion. He promised Logan wouldn't be there when I let the silence stretch on the phone. I didn't really believe him, but Benedict and Carter and Edgar and Atticus had all been kind to me, and I wanted to repay that debt while I could. Eventually, I would have to cut them all out of my life, and I didn't like to leave things unsaid.

My heart ached at the thought of not seeing Logan again, but the idea of seeing him in person, talking to him, left me utterly panicked. I dreamt of him every night, woke up crying because he wasn't there beside me. I wanted to lean into him, hug him, kiss him. Feel what it was like to actually make love to him, to feel his weight on me. I had to wipe my eyes a few times as I drove, checking in the mirror to make sure my eyes weren't red before I walked up to the house.

Hamilton greeted me at the door with a warm smile, taking my coat and ushering me into a small office on the first floor, somewhere in the depths of the house away from the kitchen. Benedict sat behind a large desk covered in piles of paper, and I raised my eyebrows as I walked in. He snorted, gesturing at a chair in front of the desk. "Don't judge me. If you knew the amount of work my brothers make for me, you'd understand the current state of my desk."

I tried a smile. "Sure." And waited.

"How are you?" Genuine concern made him look older, and he shuffled a few papers into a file folder as I cleared my throat.

"I'm fine. There was a business plan you wanted me to look at?"

He leaned over the desk and handed me the file. "Here. I'm most interested in if the costs make sense, based on what you've seen over the last couple of years, and what you think of the chef."

"The chef? Can't judge that on paper," I said, frowning as I read through the spreadsheets. My lips moved as I counted, tried to tot up the numbers in my head. Relief washed over me to know this wasn't some ridiculous trick, that this was actually about business. "Well, we spend double this amount on linen service, and that's a bargain basement number to begin with. I'm not sure how this would be possible. And triple what you've got for produce. You have to factor in spoilage."

"Good to know." He made a few notes, then handed me another stack of papers. "The chef is here to audition, so you won't have to judge him on paper. But look over the menu first, will you? We're trying for Asian fusion, whatever the fuck that is."

I smiled, even though it hurt. "It's very trendy right now." I glanced at the menu, then shrugged and handed it back. "Success depends on execution, Benedict. If you like his food, hire him. If not, keep looking. There are a lot of talented chefs out there, most of them working the line. If you need a referral, I'm happy to help."

"We should steal Jake from you."

"Go ahead and try," I said, and something close to a laugh escaped past my broken heart. "He's loyal to me only."

"Right." He got up and gestured at the door. "Would you taste the food with me? I've got peculiar tastes, I've been told, so it would be worth having your professional opinion."

I followed him, trying to think of any chefs looking for a new job. "Are you — like him?"

"Yes." Benedict cleared his throat. "I'm a lion, if that's what you mean. There are some differences, but generally — we're family, we're lions, we're alike."

A nod was all I could manage. Lions. A whole family of lions. I tried for levity, though I hugged myself. "Hunt any gazelle lately?"

"No," he said, entirely serious. "Which is too bad. Have you ever eaten gazelle, Natalia? It's delicious."

"I was joking," I said weakly.

"I wasn't." Benedict sighed, leading me down yet another hall. "It's delicious. Maybe we should start serving exotic game. There would be quite a market for gazelle and antelope and zebra. Giraffe."

I almost laughed, but I couldn't quite tell if he were joking again. "Sure. You find the supplier, I'll figure out how to cook it."

"You know, Natalia," he said, then paused. He stopped in the hall and faced me, looking too thoughtful for the clownish Benedict I'd come to appreciate. "Food means a lot to us. It does. It can be difficult to explain to others, but the sharing of a meal is a very intimate thing. It means a relationship, trust, protection. To provide a meal for someone is one of the most primitive ways of saying you care for them. To feed someone is a ... gift."

He took a deep breath, shaking his head. "It's amazing, what you do. Sharing that gift with perfect strangers. It's a little unsettling, to be perfectly honest. But when we invite someone new into our home for a meal, it means something deep."

I couldn't breathe, staring at his chest. Feeling as if he were trying to give me a serious message without actually saying it aloud, and me not really understanding. Logan invited me to cook for them, and then stay for dinner, only two days after we met. He brought me into their family before he really knew me. My heart hurt.

"Thank you," I said, patting Benedict on the arm. "I appreciate you saying that."

"Good. Just remember that when you're eating."

I frowned, following as he opened a door right next to us and went into a small dining room. It held a table set beautifully for two, complete with candles and rose petals and a fire roaring in the fireplace. A magnum of champagne cooled in a bucket next to the table. And Logan stood behind a chair, pulled out from the table, with an apprehensive, expectant look on his face.

Benedict cleared his throat and gestured at the chair. "Please sit, Ms. Spencer."

When I stared at him, my thoughts too flustered to formulate a response, he winked and then nudged me toward the chair. I stumbled a few steps but stopped, turning to look at Benedict. "But — what about the chef?"

He laughed so hard he had to catch himself against the wall. I looked at Logan, who was also smiling, and back at Benedict. Benedict leaned forward to seize my head and kiss my forehead. "Christ, you're funny. Logan's your chef, Natalia. He's auditioning."

"Oh." Still stunned, I looked at Logan. He wore a suit, charcoal pinstripe with a lavender shirt and matching patterned tie. Silver cufflinks winked in the candlelight. I looked behind me as the door shut with a click, then back at Logan. My face heated and I wanted to melt into a puddle of sheer humiliation. "I'm so sorry, I don't —"

"Just sit for a bit, Natalia."

The way he said my name made my knees weak, and I could not have said how grateful I was for the hand he offered, leading me around the table to take my seat. His hands drifted across my shoulders, and I desperately wished I'd worn something nicer than jeans and a sweater and cowboy boots.

Logan sat in the chair next to me, still holding my hand. He stared at me like he could drink me in, like he needed to memorize every detail about me. "I did actually cook. He wasn't joking about that part."

"Oh." I seemed to be saying that a lot. I cleared my throat, looking around the room to distract myself as his eyes turned to molten copper. "This is a nice room. Do you — use it often?"

"Not often." He stroked the back of my hand. "I know I scared you, Natalia. I know — what I am is not something you understand or even want to understand. But the last month has been an eternity of misery for me. I need you in my life."

My heart leapt, but a frisson of fear slid through me. He was still a lion. "I've been miserable, too." The traitorous words slipped out before I could bite them back.

Before he could speak, the door opened and Atticus walked in, carrying two bowls of soup. He put them down in front of us and went down to one knee next to my chair. Panic rose up and I almost jumped out of my chair. Atticus, the giant bruiser of an enforcer, looked at me and said, "Natalia, you make my brother very happy. I give you this food and ask you to join our family. Please eat, and find strength, and be warm."

He got up, turned on his heel, and walked out. The door clicked shut behind him.

I stared at the door, then at Logan. He smiled at me and started eating. Stumped, I did the same. It was some sort of pumpkin puree, well seasoned and spiced, creamy and warm and delicious. We ate, and he held my hand, now and then squeezing my fingers with his.

When I put the spoon down, I dabbed my mouth with the napkin and glanced at the fire. "Benedict said you cooked this yourself?"

"I have some secrets, believe it or not." Logan smiled easily, looking relaxed. Content. He poured more champagne into my flute, clinking his glass against mine. "I know my way around a kitchen when I have a recipe to follow. I'm not as creative as you are, though."

"I don't know about —" I cut off as the door opened again. Atticus retrieved the soup bowls, but before I could ask him what he'd meant, Carter arrived with the salad.

Carter looked nervous, smiling widely at me as he put the plates in front of us. Then he, too, dropped to one knee next to my chair and looked at me earnestly. "Natalia, you make my brother very happy. I give you this food and ask you to join our family. Please eat, and find strength, and be warm."

Then he grinned, got up, and disappeared.

I put my hands over my face, almost undone by the kindness. "You have got to tell me what's going on."

"I did it wrong," he said at length. He picked through the salad, a lovely tangle of spinach and strawberries and goat cheese and candied pecans. "When I asked you to be with me. I forgot that you're joining a family, not just a couple. My brothers gave me hell for scaring you off. They wanted a chance to tell you that you are appreciated and loved. That even when I am not there, they will be there to support and protect you."

I cleared my throat through a knot of tears, hating that I was going to cry again. I never cried, and yet this man and his brothers had me a mess with a dozen words or less. Plus tears made it almost impossible to enjoy the salad or the champagne.

He asked me about the restaurant and Ruby, casual conversation as if it were a normal date instead of some weird audition to join his family. And still I wanted to know what Benedict would bring. Probably trouble, if the past were any indication.

Carter took away the salad plates and Benedict entered on his heels, carrying two plates with beautiful pork medallions, sautéed greens, and what looked like a grape sauce. It smelled heavenly. He poured more champagne for us both, then dropped to both knees. Benedict spread his arms wide and declared, "Natalia, you made my asshole brother very happy. Really, he's completely unbearable when you're not here. I give you this food and hope to God you'll agree to join our family. Please choke it down, and find strength, and be warm. And be patient, and beautiful, and kind. You'll need all those things if you expect to —"

Logan aimed a kick in his direction and Benedict jumped up, looking injured. "Do you see what we have to put up with? Dear Natalia, you soothe the savage beast. Do us a favor and agree to soothe him a couple times tonight and again in the morning." Then he winked and whistled his way out the door.

I laughed as the door closed, and Logan pinched the bridge of his nose, obviously long-suffering with his brother's tomfoolery. Something bubbled up in my chest, something happy and excited. Something that believed this might actually work. That I could live with a lion. But I focused on my plate, closing my eyes as I inhaled the steam. "This is lovely. You made this?"

"Mostly." He frowned, tasting the sauce. "I asked Hamilton to grill the pork, so it was fresh when we ate. But the grape sauce, that's mine."

I made yummy noises and he snorted. "Don't patronize me, master chef."

"Believe me, I wouldn't be eating it if I didn't like it." I pointed my fork at him. "Life's too short to eat flavorless food."

"Amen." Logan demolished his meal and sat back to watch as I savored mine. The pork was tender and salty, balanced by the sweet tang of the grape reduction, and the bitterness of the sautéed kale gentled with lemon and garlic.

I had to pause to breathe and instead sipped from the champagne, letting the bubbles tickle my nose. I felt almost giddy. "Why are you doing this?"

Logan's eyebrows arched. "Isn't it obvious?"

"Humor me."

The skin around his eyes crinkled as he smiled. "Natalia, I love you. I love you so much there aren't words for it. My lion loves you, he yearns for you. You're a constant refrain in the back of my head. I want to feed you, to protect you, to keep you in my bed."

I shivered at the memory of being in my bed together, not just when he touched me and I touched him, but when I was afraid and he held me close and woke me from nightmares. "I just don't know if I can — deal with what you are. The lion thing."

"The lion *king*," he said, and I laughed.

But I paused. "Wait. Are you a lion king?"

He laughed hard enough to jostle the table and my champagne almost tipped. He filled it back up, shaking his head. "Not exactly. But we can talk more about that later. All I'm asking is that you give us a chance."

I stared past his shoulder, gripping my thighs as I tried to balance the romance of the meal and the lovely things his brothers said with the cold reality of him turning into an animal. A predator. More champagne seemed like a good idea, and I let it slide down my throat. "What's for dessert?"

As if on cue, Benedict returned to whirl away the dinner plates, and then Edgar approached with a single bowl of fluffy chocolate mousse. Two spoons. A dollop of fresh whipped cream on top and a bowl of cut strawberries. Edgar, grave and dignified, eased to one knee and looked up at me. My breath caught and for some reason, his gaze made me want to cry.

Edgar's gravelly voice reached me from very far away. "Natalia. You make my brother very happy. I give you this food and ask you to join our family. Please eat. Find your strength. Be warmed. Be safe." He squeezed my knee as he stood, but instead of departing, he took a deep breath and added, "You make each other better. If that isn't love, I don't know what is."

Then he was gone.

Even Logan looked a little surprised, but then he picked up a strawberry, dipped it in the mousse, and held it out to me. When I reached for it, he pulled back, eyebrows raised. I flushed, opened my mouth. He placed the strawberry against my lips, smeared a little chocolate across them, and then pushed it into my mouth. My heart beat very fast, pounded against my ribs. I savored the strawberry, the chocolate, the feeling of his thumb against my lip. My fingers trembled as I picked up a strawberry and covered it in chocolate, then offered it to him.

Logan smiled, leaned closer, and opened his mouth. I rested it against his tongue and caught my breath as he held my wrist. Ate the strawberry and then licked the juice off my fingers. Desire shivered through me and landed in my center. He kissed my palm, then the inside of my wrist. "Do you love me, Natalia?"

"Yes." I breathed the word, almost in a trance.

He smiled, and some of the weight lifted off his shoulders, and he looked younger, more at ease. He fed me another strawberry but was messier, left chocolate across my mouth, and leaned in to lick it off, kissing me deeply, intensely. Until he bit my lower lip and I nearly jumped out of my chair, holding on to his face to keep his mouth against mine. God help me.

"Will you live with me?"

I closed my eyes, pressed soft kisses against his lips over and over, then across his cheek. Melted against him. "Yes."

I felt his smile rather than saw it, then his arms crushed me to him and the dessert was forgotten. Which was really too bad, because it was delicious.

chapter 17

The meal went better than he hoped, and though he didn't expect her to agree, his heart leapt when she said she loved him. It took all his strength not to wipe all the dishes from the table and spread her across the top of it to really kiss. Instead, he picked her up and carried her out of the dining room and toward his suite. He ignored the rowdy cheers from down the hall, particularly as Natalia stopped nibbling at his jaw to look over his shoulder. "What was that?"

"I'm sure they're watching a football game," he said, not wanting to spook her.

She raised an eyebrow. "A football game where we fuck at the end?"

He laughed but didn't answer, only kicking open the door to his suite and kicking it closed behind him. Then it was a short walk to the bedroom. He'd started a fire there and changed the sheets to the high quality cotton ones —

just in case things went well. Logan dropped Natalia on the mattress and stood over her, just looking at her. Drinking her in.

She went up on her elbows, eyebrow raised. "What?"

"You're just — too beautiful."

"I know." She sat and tugged on his tie, then pulled his shirt out of his pants and reached for his belt.

Logan pinned her back against the bed, kissing her until she sighed and moved against him. He undressed her, starting with a pair of ridiculous cowboy boots. Threw them aside, then unbuttoned her jeans and tugged them down her long, muscled legs. He picked up her foot and kissed her ankle, trailed kisses up to her knee.

Her eyes had gone dark with desire as she sprawled across his bed. Logan dropped her leg and instead tugged her shirt over her head, burying his face between her breasts as soon as they were revealed. She laughed but pulled impatiently at his shirt. "You should be naked too. I want to see you."

"Do you?" His voice went all throaty and deep, the lion shivering to the surface because he wanted her so desperately his control nearly slipped.

She bit her lower lip, a hint of a smile escaping.

He almost came just from that look. He rubbed her thigh as he stood between her knees, taking in the smooth expanse of pale skin, the lacy bra that still hid her breasts. She looked soft and warm and ready. Willing. Just waiting for him to claim her. Logan took off his tie and jacket, threw them onto the chair in the corner, then pulled off his shirt. Stretched for her benefit, and even flexed a little. Just because.

Natalia stroked her stomach, watching him. "Lose the pants."

He laced his hands behind his head and raised an eyebrow at her. "Go ahead."

"Lazy kitty," she murmured, sitting up and taking his belt in hand. She unbuckled it, worked the button and then the zipper. Her hands pushed the pants from his hips, then she ran a finger under the waist of his boxer briefs. Teased him, looking up with wide eyes as she batted her eyelashes. "Do you have something in there for me?"

Logan caught a handful of her hair and dragged her face to his for a kiss, crushing her lips and thrusting his tongue into her mouth. She would learn that lions didn't like to be teased. She melted in his arms, let the force of his kiss bear her back to the mattress, and Logan pushed her higher on the bed. He kept his grip on her hair, though, as he slid his hand into her panties. Found her wet and wanting, his fingers sliding easily into her crease. Natalia moaned and arched against him, her nails dragged across his chest.

He kissed her again, then tore off the bra that still concealed her perfect breasts. Her nipples stood out, pink and dainty. Logan circled one with his tongue, sucked on her nipple and then her entire breast, pulling deeply enough that she cried out and grabbed his hair. He lifted his head, loving the erotic flush traveling up her throat to her cheeks and the tangle of her dark hair against his pillows. He could watch her all night. Every night. For the rest of his life.

"I love the way you moan," he said, then bit her lip.

Natalia looked a little dazed, reaching for him. "Kiss me again."

"I will." Logan chuckled and slid down her body, dragging the panties away until he breathed against the heated skin at the apex of her thighs. Kissed her there and reveled in the taste of her, the quick, breathy moans she made, the way she grabbed his hair but squeezed her breast at the same time. "Come for me, baby."

Her hips pushed at his face, and he had to pin her thighs down, working steadily to bring to the edge of orgasm just before he backed off. She hovered; he felt the ripples in her core as he teased her clit in delicate, soft, brief touches. Natalia reached down to finish herself, growling in frustration, but Logan knocked her hands away. He nibbled along the inside of her thigh, letting his beard scrape against the sensitive skin. "You want something?"

"I want you." Her head tossed on the pillow and her hips bucked, she pushed at him and begged. "Please. I want to feel you."

He groaned, his cock ready to explode at the thought of her silky channel, but dragged off his briefs as he latched his mouth to her clit and sucked. Hard. The scream started low in her throat but built, and then she wailed, arching away from the mattress and grabbing double handfuls of the sheets as tremors rolled through her. Logan had never seen anything so beautiful in his entire life.

A sheen of sweat covered her, covered him as well as he knelt between her thighs. He pinned her shoulders down and nuzzled his nose against hers. "Ready?"

It took her forever to open her eyes, glazed and dazed from her orgasm, and she stroked his cheek with a sigh. "Go slow. I want to feel you."

It took all his control not to take her hard, right then. She'd feel that. But there was time for that later, when they knew each other better. He held his weight off her, taking his cock in hand to rub the head through the slick heat of her pussy. Natalia moaned and lifted her hips. "More."

"Bossy little thing, aren't you?" He kissed her into silence so he could press the tip into her in peace, and her body clutched him in a warm, wet embrace. He slid deeper and she sighed, broke the kiss to make a soft little "Oooh" sound that branded itself on his brain. Her body rolled against his, hips tilting, and Logan groaned, thrusting until his stomach met hers, and he was in.

She made that sighing, hungry sound, like the yummy noises when she ate, and he held still until she settled. Her legs lifted, wrapped around his hips, and she stroked the back of his neck. Natalia's blue eyes found his in the firelight. "You feel so good, Logan."

He started moving, slow and steady, until those little sighs turned deeper, into moans. He stroked through her, watching the flush rise in her cheeks again, the sweat beading on her forehead. Until she froze underneath him, meeting his thrusts with short little jerks of her own, and her muscles squeezed his cock and the pressure built in his balls until he couldn't wait, he couldn't stop. He moved faster, harder, thrusting until the slapping of their flesh filled the room, until the wet sounds of his body filling hers deafened him and control was a distant memory.

He pinned her shoulder down with one hand and tilted her hips up with the other, deepening the penetration until she cried out again and again and clawed at his sides. And still the lion wanted more. Needed more. He pulled out abruptly and flipped her onto her stomach, pulling her hips up and plunging back into her before she could do more than get her hands underneath her.

Logan leaned over her back, his arm a bar across her chest to keep from fucking her into the headboard, and growled. She cried out, pushing back to meet him, and he grabbed her hips, yanking her back into every thrust. Fucking her until she seized up again and he had to force his way through her spasming channel until — release. His balls exploded and he filled her in a heated rush, kept thrusting until his come spilled out and down her thighs. She moaned low in her throat and collapsed forward onto the pillows, panting.

He stayed deep in her, never wanting to leave her, and lay on his side with her tight against his chest. He closed his eyes and struggled for breath, stroking her stomach over and over as she sighed and trembled, and aftershocks rippled through her core every time he moved. Logan kissed her shoulder, right where he would bite her if he meant to turn her, and hoped his voice sounded normal. "Are you okay?"

She stretched with a little wince, but sighed, so close to that delicious "oooh" she made that he was immediately hard again. She looked over her shoulder at him, then down at where they remained joined. "Better than okay?"

He laughed and eased back, let her lay on her back so he could move over her again. "I'll take it easy this time." He licked the sweat off her chest, between her breasts, and her fingers worked into his hair. "Unless you have other ideas?"

She smiled, then sat up to push him onto his back. "I might."

My arms and legs still didn't cooperate as I wiggled out from under him and nudged Logan onto his back. His hands trailed along my sides, sending shivers through me, and the heat in his gaze lit another fire in my center. I wanted him so much I couldn't look away as I straddled his thighs, afraid if I looked away he would disappear or turn into a dream. That I would wake up and I'd still be at my apartment, depressed and alone without him.

I bit my lower lip as I settled on his thighs, not quite ready to brave another round with his massive cock. The unbelievable fullness from his first entry still sent delicious ripples through me, but every inch of my skin was hypersensitive. He held my knees, trying to pull me closer, and I braced my hands on his chest. Leaned forward so I could kiss him and feel the hard heat of his body against my stomach. I murmured, "We need some rules, Logan."

He gazed up at me, golden eyes dreamy as he stroked my back, and his hips lifted to push at me. "Rules?"

As if he had no idea what the word meant.

I tried to control the lust as another little moan slipped out, as his tongue slipped into my mouth and teased the desire to an inferno. He still tasted a little like chocolate and strawberries. I slid one hand into his long hair and pulled his face away. "Rules," I said, voice unsteady. "No controlling asshole behavior, got it? I make my own decisions."

"Sounds good, no objections," he said, arms tightening around me as he tried to kiss me again. He nibbled on my chin and stroked along my ribs. "Just let me —"

I planted a hand on his chest and sat back, heart fluttering and racing at the same time. Holy Christ, the man was my undoing. One touch and I lost all sense. But I couldn't stop touching him. Or myself. The way his eyes devoured my body, the way he reached for me — I stroked my stomach, my breasts, thinking of the way he wanted me.

"And I'm staying human," I said, swallowing the nerves at such a declaration. What if he decided to bite me anyway? Would I lose my humanity for him? "Until we talk more."

"We can talk more later," he said. Logan took himself in hand and stroked his cock, watching as I played with my nipples. A low growl rumbled through him and vibrated against me in the best possible way. "But I won't bite you. Not until you ask me to." He chuckled.

"Okay." My head tilted back and I couldn't for the life of me remember what I wanted to say. Couldn't have been that important. I eased up, and he rubbed the head of his cock against my clit, and my legs failed. I sank down on him and moaned as he filled me. The hard heat of his body ignited fire inside mine and he moved, couldn't stop moving as he thrust up and up and up, and I tried to meet his urgency with my own.

Lightning sparked around me as I rode him, orgasm rolling through me as I moved and couldn't stop, as he grabbed my hips and dragged my mouth to his. I seized up, shaking as I came, but Logan continued on and on until I lay boneless atop him.

He kissed my neck, and his teeth grazed along my shoulder as his arms tightened and captured me, as his hips jerked and the rush of his release poured into me. He cried out with me, as my nails raked down his sides, and then the only sound was panting breath and a raspy growl from him.

Logan kept kissing me as the aftershocks subsided and his body slipped from mine. He drew me close to his side, though, and pulled the sheets up over us. He kissed along my forehead, down my cheek to my ear and jaw, as if he needed to map and taste every part of me. I looked forward to it immensely.

I sighed and rested my head on his chest, eyes closed. "Don't think for a second I'll let you tell me what to do at the restaurant."

He laughed, bouncing me around, then grumbled and kissed me more. "Not at the restaurant, agreed. Does that mean I can tell you what to do everywhere else? In bed?"

"We can talk about that later," I said, flushing.

"Oh yes." His voice got all deep and I shivered in anticipation.

At least life with a lion wouldn't be boring.

epilogue

The dinner rush slammed the kitchen. I juggled two orders of the house special, one of which went to a serious food critic and the other to her husband, when one of the servers poked his head into the kitchen with a grin. "Chef?"

I didn't look up from plating the braised lamb. "Yeah?"

"A guest wants to speak with you."

Shit. I wiped my hands off on my apron and gestured for Jake to take over, thinking only of that damn critic. If she didn't like us, we'd be dead in the water for at least a couple of months. Despite Carter saying we made a lot more money than I thought, I didn't trust it. Didn't trust the numbers. We weren't a success yet. At least, we weren't *enough* of a success.

I chewed my lip and followed him out of the kitchen, noting the smiles on the staff's faces but not registering what they had to be so pleased about — I snapped, "Mind that béarnaise, and if you burn the béchamel, you're washing dishes for a week" over my shoulder as the door swung shut.

The dining room bustled with activity, conversation and laughter and clinking dishes filled it with a happy noise. I remembered what Benedict told me about how special it was to feed people, how intimate a gift. It made me smile as I wiped my hands over and over on my towel, a nervous habit from school I still hadn't broken.

But instead of stopping at the food critic's table, the waiter led me to the round table near the front where three men sat. I folded my arms over my chest and tried to scowl as the server giggled and disappeared, his mission complete, and I whacked Benedict with my towel. "And what the hell do *you* want?"

"It was him," the lawyer said, laughing, and pointed at Logan.

"I'm too busy for this silliness," I said. I pointed at the kitchen behind me but couldn't hide a stupid smile that seemed to take up permanent residence on my face whenever Logan was around. "I have meals to prepare. There's a very special guest here tonight, and we *have* to make a good impression."

"I just had a question about my steak," Logan said, low and slow and with his eyes half-closed.

Fuck. That. I leveled a glare at him. "Don't —"

"Come here." He peered at the steak. "I thought I saw something on it."

"You're full of shit." But I edged around the table, within his reach, and gave Edgar a look. "I thought you were supposed to keep him in line?"

The security chief shrugged and threw his hands in the air. "I'm only one man."

The moment I was close enough and distracted by the steak, which really did have something strange next to it, Logan captured me around the waist. Drew me into his lap as I squawked and flailed, and he kissed me to silence. There were a few whistles and claps from our regular clientele, who'd all witnessed similar interactions over the past few weeks. I refused to admit how happy it made me that Logan couldn't keep his hands off me. The moment I got within a few feet of him, he had to touch me — had to hold my hand, or brush my neck, or kiss my cheek. He gave me goosebumps every time.

Logan looped his arms around my waist. "Seriously. There's something on my steak."

Despite that my stomach clenched at the feel of his hard thighs under mine, I frowned at the plate. Then moved the steak with his fork and saw... a ring. A simple platinum band with an enormous diamond. A diamond. An odd sound, maybe a croak, escaped my throat.

Logan kissed my neck, moving me to his chair as he went to one knee, murmuring, "I wonder how that got there."

My vision blurred until I couldn't see anything — and certainly not that gorgeous ring. And Logan held my hand as cheers erupted from the restaurant and the kitchen, and he said beautiful, wonderful things that I only half-heard, too stunned to do or say anything as he held up the ring and asked me to marry him.

I could only nod, crying and laughing as he put the meat-scented ring on my finger and then rose, lifted me up in a tight embrace and spun me around. And kissed me until the world blurred and I didn't give a shit about the dinner rush. He held me up as my knees wobbled and I almost fell, pressing my face against his chest. His head bent so he could whisper through the din of the celebrating restaurant. "You can make my steak any way you want, Natalia, as long as it's forever. Say it's forever."

"Forever," I said, and kissed him back.

Then Benedict and Edgar and Carter and Atticus broke out magnums of champagne for the entire restaurant, announcing the meals were on the house to celebrate, and the toasts went on for what seemed like hours, until I was twirly-headed and dazzled and so in love I almost couldn't stand. And Logan was there to support me when I needed it, and he let me shine when the critic came to congratulate me and offer her compliments on the food. The entire night passed in a blur, and most of the next day passed in a haze of champagne and strawberries and chocolate and sex.

The restaurant got a hell of a write-up in the paper, and not even Logan could get reservations in under a month. Luckily, we kept a table in the kitchen just for family.

a sneak peak:

chasing trouble

Benedict hated getting up early on his day off. He'd been looking forward to a lazy Friday of sweatpants, grilled cheese sandwiches, and beer. Until Atticus called. From jail.

He gritted his teeth as he strode into the reception area. It would take a couple of hours to sort this all out, though Benedict didn't have his hopes up. Atticus hadn't been particularly forthcoming about what led to his arrest, and the sullen "I don't knows" felt more like teenage angst than what a goddamn man would own up to.

Benedict knew the clerks and bailiffs at the jail and the courthouse, and smiled and joked about being there on unofficial official business as the morning ticked away. All while wanting to punch Atticus in the face the moment he saw him. The feeling intensified when he paid out the ten thousand dollar bond to the clerk, gritting his teeth as he imagined all the ways to make Atticus pay it back. Son of a bitch.

The deputies brought Atticus out and for a moment Benedict couldn't speak — his little brother looked like hell warmed over, even with their supernatural healing ability. Bruises and lumps covered his face and at least two massive cuts had butterfly bandages holding them together. Benedict raised his eyebrows as he pointed Atticus into the corner. "Over there. Sit."

Atticus scrubbed a hand over his short hair, holding his bag of belongings from the property locker. "Can't we do this at home? I feel like shit."

"You look worse, and we're doing this here so I can decide what to tell Logan." Benedict scanned the handful of other people waiting in the reception area; all human, nothing to worry about. He loomed over Atticus as the younger man flopped into a flimsy plastic chair that creaked dangerously under his weight. "What the fuck is wrong with you?"

"There was a fight, the cops showed up, I tried to shift and get away but ended up naked in an alley. They used their imaginations. Nothing I could do about it."

"Why the fuck were you naked in an alley?" Benedict heard a snort behind him and lowered his voice, fury swelling his shoulders as the lion wanted to burst forth and teach his brother a lesson.

Atticus shrugged, not meeting his gaze but staring past Benedict at the door. A muscle jumped in his jaw, just under a thick white scar from his ear to his throat. "It just happened."

Benedict massaged his temples and turned away for a moment so he wouldn't grab the kid by the throat and throw him across the room. *It just happened.* It always just happened around Atticus. It was the fourth time in as many months that he'd been arrested for fighting, or public nudity, or any number of minor crimes. Enough that Logan was starting to get pissed.

Benedict took a deep breath and faced his brother. "You have got to get this under control. I don't know what the fuck you're doing, Atticus, but clean it up. Got me?"

"I get it." The sullenness faded to fatigue, and for a moment Benedict saw his brother exhausted, beaten. Broken. Atticus gingerly put his head in his hands. "I don't know if I can stop."

"We'll figure it out." Benedict didn't fully understand what the problem was, just that his brother needed help. Something was seriously wrong, and if—

He turned as slow-moving chaos burst into the reception area, two patrol cops wrestling with a kid and getting a little too rough. Benedict frowned, gesturing at his brother to get up and handing him the keys. "Let's get you some food and —"

"I'm innocent," the kid yowled, and the hair stood up on Benedict's arms. His vision narrowed, focused on the kid, and he saw her face. Not a kid, a young woman. Being manhandled far too roughly, unprofessionally, by two cops who enjoyed it a bit too much. She looked ill, weak, and kept her eyes screwed shut as she struggled. "Let me go, you're not supposed to —"

"Shut the fuck up," one of the cops said, grabbing a fistful of her hair and knocking the girl over one of those damn plastic chairs.

Atticus bristled, growled a little, and Benedict shoved him at the door. "I'll handle it, you don't need to get arrested again. *Go.*"

And Benedict strode forward. "Hey! Get your hands off my client before I file excessive force and brutality complaints."

The cops scowled but eased up; one held the girl's upper arm as the other handed the arrest paperwork to booking. One muttered, "Your client? She must account for half your salary."

"Unhand my client." Fear rolled off the girl in waves and riled up his lion, along with the cruelty emanating from the cops. Benedict had a healthy respect for the police but wouldn't tolerate the occasional bad seeds that turned up in their line of work. He looked past the cops at the booking agent and tilted his head at a few chairs in a more private corner. "Do you mind if I speak with my client briefly? We'll be filing the bail agreement shortly."

The clerk smiled, clicking away at the computer. "Of course, Benedict. We'll have her processed lickety-split."

"Good." He caught the girl's elbow and pulled her away from the handsy cop, scowling at the dick as they moved away. In the corner, Benedict put the girl in one of the chairs and placed himself between her and the cops, so they couldn't see her and she couldn't see them. He kept his voice low enough they wouldn't overhear. "What's your name?"

"Eloise."

Her voice was low and throaty, and she kept her eyes on the floor. A frisson of interest, of curiosity, ran through him. The tone in her voice, the smell of her skin, and the crackle in the air around her meant non-human. Definitely something supernatural, but she didn't smell like a lion or a wolf or any shifter he knew. He took a deep breath near her and the girl went still, sliding a glance at him. Ice blue eyes, almost silver, slid across his face and then back to the floor. They hit him like a punch in the gut, and he forgot, for a moment, where he was.

He shook himself back to reality. Time was limited and he had to get her away from the jail before she ended up booked all weekend. "I'm Benedict. I'll be your lawyer for the time being, at least until we can get you out of here."

"Great." She picked at a loose thread on her jeans, hands nervous despite the handcuffs restraining her.

"What did they pick you up for?"

She made an odd noise in her throat, almost a laugh, but shrugged instead. "They didn't really say."

Irritated, Benedict spun on his heel and confronted the cops. "What are the charges against my client?"

The taller cop, unimpressed, raised his eyebrows and handed over a copy of the arrest sheet. "Oh, you know. Small potatoes. Illegal betting, book making, money laundering, fraudulent wire transfers, and some racketeering."

"Racketeering?" Benedict took the paper but didn't look away from the cop. "Are you fucking kidding me? Does she look capable of racketeering?" And he flung his arm back at the girl, who blinked and looked around as if confused why she was even at the jail.

The short cop snorted, an ugly sound. "Look, friend, you don't know your client very well. We've arrested her at least ten times this year alone. Theft, transporting stolen goods, forgery, obstructing an official investigation, breaking and entering... You're not getting out of this shit," and he pointed at Eloise behind Benedict. "These are federal charges, sweetheart, so you best pay your lawyer however you can."

And the sneer on his face left little doubt how he thought Eloise paid him. Benedict's blood ran cold with rage and his lion roared in the back of his head, ready to pounce. But he kept his face expressionless as he looked at the patrol cops. "If you have any issues, address them to me. My client will not be speaking with you further."

He looked at the girl and the curtain of dark hair hiding her expression. He dropped his voice again as the cops headed for the door. "Forgery? Really?"

A hint of a smile, quickly hidden. "No idea what they're talking about."

Benedict snorted, about to go back to the clerk to resolve the bail, then leaned down to try to see her face. "Who are your people?"

She went very still. Her gaze slowly lifted to his face and Benedict rocked back on his heels; definitely supernatural. Had to be. Her eyes were gray-silver with hints of blue, flecks of lightning through the irises. Enthralling. Devastating.

She cleared her throat. "I'm Eloise. That's it."

A mystery. His lion perked up. He grinned, patted her shoulder. "What are you doing for lunch?"

About the Author

Thank you for reading! I hope you enjoyed the City Shifters books. If you'd like to be notified of new releases, please join my mailing list by going to EEPURL.COM/BWQZ3X

Please feel free to email me directly at
LAYLARNASH@YAHOO.COM

or check out my website at
LAYLANASH.COM.

If you enjoyed the book, please take a moment to leave a review. I'd love to hear from you!

Thanks!
Layla

Also by Layla Nash

City Shifters: the Pride
Thrill of the Chase
Chasing Trouble
Storm Chaser
Cut to the Chase
Chasing the Dream
A Chase Christmas
A Valentine's Chase

City Shifters: the Den
Bearing Burdens
Bearing Hearts
Bearing Scars
Bearing Demons
Bearing Secrets

Other Paranormal Romance
His Bear Hands (with Callista Ball)

Made in the USA
Monee, IL
14 May 2020

30937023R00106